D1324903

'Go back to the city where you belong,'
ordered Kelly Sinclair contemptuously
when Paige made an impulsive journey
from Sydney to the outback. And
Paige would by then have been only
too glad to oblige—she didn't want
to be in this disagreeable man's company any longer than she could help
—but fate forestalled her, with disastrous results . . .

BINDABURRA OUTSTATION

BY
KERRY ALLYNE

MILLS & BOON LIMITED
LONDON W1

*First published 1980
Australian copyright 1980
Philippine copyright 1980
This edition 1980*

© Kerry Allyne 1980

ISBN 0 263 73279 7

Set in Linotype Baskerville 10 on 12 pt.

*Made and printed in Great Britain by
Richard Clay (The Chaucer Press), Ltd., Bungay, Suffolk*

CHAPTER ONE

Now that the torrential rain had eased and the parting clouds were allowing the glittering shine of a few stars to be seen, Paige stepped past the open doorway of the bar in Tingala's single hotel and decided on a tour of inspection of the town. Not that there was much to see, it consisted of only one wide and sparsely settled street, but after three days confined at the wheel of her Volkswagen she felt the distinct need for some exercise.

Until she had run into the downpour this afternoon her long journey to the outback had been quite uneventful. Interesting, in that she had been seeing a part of the country she had always wanted to visit, but uneventful nonetheless. However, with the coming of the storm while she was still some fifty miles out of town that had all changed, and to such an extent that at one stage she had worriedly believed she wasn't going to make it to Tingala at all. As the rain continued to fall the red soil road had developed disconcerting quagmire qualities which had at times come close to bogging her car irretrievably.

Carefully watching where she trod in order to avoid the water-filled potholes which abounded in the street, Paige only managed to make her way slowly past the next two buildings before coming to the conclusion

that she was wasting her time. When it was wet that
thick layer of fine bulldust was almost as difficult for
man to traverse as it was for machines. It squelched
stickily around her shoes every time she took a step
and, to her dismay, she discovered it was surprisingly
slippery. She had nearly lost her footing and fallen
ignominiously in the mud a couple of times already.

With a wry grimace for the lost opportunity to stretch
her legs she hitched her navy slacks higher to keep
them out of harm's way and cautiously headed back to
the hotel's wooden verandah, where she proceeded to
make use of the old boot-scraper which had been left
outside for just such an occasion.

'Too messy for walking, was it?' asked a commiserat-
ing voice as a broad figure came to stand in the doorway, peering out at the particularly clouded heavens.

'Just a little,' Paige agreed, her mobile mouth curving
into a rueful smile as she glanced up at the hotel's
sociable proprietor. 'I could see myself falling flat on
my back if I tried to make it to the end of the street,
so I decided to turn back. Is it always like this when
it rains?' Her head tilted to one side questioningly.

'So I believe,' he nodded wryly. 'I'm a relative new-
comer to the area myself—only been here a few months
—but they say it doesn't take much to close the roads
in these parts.'

'I will still be able to get through to Greenvale Station tomorrow, though, won't I?' she queried immediately, disappointed lest she had come so far only to
be thwarted within striking distance of her objective.
'Now that the rain seems to be moving on there
shouldn't be any more trouble with the roads, should
there?'

His shoulders lifted in a gesture of ignorance. 'I really couldn't say for certain, lass. I haven't done much travelling in that direction, so I don't know what the conditions are likely to be.' A frown settled on his forehead at being unable to offer more assistance and then suddenly cleared as he exclaimed, 'But there's someone here who *could* tell you. He came in this afternoon to collect supplies for Bindaburra Outstation, and that's only forty or fifty miles from where you want to go. I'll get him to have a word with you,' he offered cheerily, and before Paige could even begin to thank him had promptly begun to call back towards the bar. 'Kelly! Kelly Sinclair! Can you spare a moment? There's someone here who wants to speak to you.'

From within the building came the sound of a chair being pushed back, followed by heavy footsteps crossing to the hall.

'Wants to speak to me?' The man who emerged from the room enquired frowningly. 'What about?'

'The roads north of here,' his host supplied with a grin, and thereby giving Paige time to take stock of her anticipated informant as he moved to join them.

Tall and ruggedly built, he was dressed in close-fitting moleskins which sat low on slim hips and out-lined the powerful length of strongly muscled legs, while a weatherproof jacket hung open to reveal a broad chest covered by a blue checked shirt. Beneath thick black hair the face which scrutinised Paige in return was coolly alert and dissecting. Clear blue-grey eyes gleamed startlingly against the dark hue of his skin in the light of the hall, and above the firm tenacious line of his jaw a wryly shaped mouth sat at odds with the rest of his uncompromising appearance.

'Who wants to know?' he drawled, his eyes never wavering from the expectant face before him.

'I do, Mr Sinclair,' Paige spoke up quickly, sweeping a rusty red fall of hair back from her cheek with a nervous hand. That assessing gaze of his was slightly discomposing. 'My name's Paige Darling, and—and I was hoping to get through to Greenvale Station tomorrow. Mr Johnson,' she indicated the rather rotund man who was just proffering his apologies and returning to the bar in response to a customer's hail, 'suggested I should ask you if it would be possible.'

'Not unless you've got a four-wheel-drive vehicle it won't be,' he shrugged with what could only be described as complete indifference.

'Oh, but surely the roads will have improved by tomorrow,' she persevered stoutly. 'I mean, the rain's gone now, hasn't it?'

'Has it?' One very dark eyebrow tilted expressively.

Emerald green eyes searched the increasingly star-studded sky with some asperity. 'Well, hasn't it?' she asked again, only a little more sharply this time.

'No, Miss Darling, it has not,' he returned lazily, the subtle inflection he placed on her surname sending a warm flush surging into her cheeks. Abruptly, his long-lashed eyes narrowed shrewdly. 'What's the great attraction at the Thorntons' property, anyway? Stuart?'

Paige's smooth skin took on a even more fiery tint. 'That's none of your concern, Mr Sinclair!' she flared, then went on to gibe with a scorn totally foreign to her normal nature, 'I'm not in the habit of discussing my private business with—what are you?—an overseer... a stockman ... a station hand?'

Apart from a perceptible outthrust of his unyielding chin, her words appeared to have little, if any, effect on the man confronting her. 'While I'm working on Binda-burra I guess you could probably say I'm a mixture of all three,' she was advised steadily.

Already regretting her previous deprecatory tone, Paige embarrassedly set out to make amends. 'Yes, well, I'm sorry I spoke to you like I did. Actually I was in-vited to visit Greenvale for the annual Picnic Races and the Grand Ball which follows. A whole crowd of us were, when Stuart came to one of my cousin's parties in Sydney a couple of months ago.'

'But you were the only one to take up his invitation?'

The observation was pointedly made and Paige shifted her stance, inexplicably uncomfortable. 'Origi-nally it was intended that four of us would come, but the others—er—dropped out at the last minute,' she explained.

'Not you, though?' His lips twisted a little grimly.

'I couldn't see any reason why I should,' she coun-tered, recovering her composure and raising her head challengingly higher. 'I'd always wanted to see what it was like in this part of the State and this seemed a perfect opportunity to do so.'

'And now you've made the trip for nothing.' His expression was one of doubtful sympathy.

'Oh, I don't know.' She hunched her shoulders airily. 'There's still another week till the races are due to be held. I might just stay in Tingala for a few days and then continue on to Greenvale.'

'In another few days I doubt whether you'll be able to leave Tingala—for Greenvale—or anywhere else for that matter.'

'Because, according to you, there's going to be more rain?' she laughed, openly sceptical. With the sky clearing by the minute she couldn't possibly see his prediction coming true. He was just trying to be difficult! 'But you came in to town on those roads this afternoon, Mr Sinclair, so why can't I go out on them just as easily tomorrow, hmm?'

'Because, Miss Darling, *that* happens to be the transport I used.' Kelly pointed out a mud-encrusted Land Cruiser partially visible at the side of the hotel. 'Now, suppose you tell me how you think your car measures up against one of those over-flooded and almost non-existent roads, *hmm?*'

'Flooded?' Paige's finely marked brows arched sardonically. 'I didn't see any creeks or causeways even approaching that condition in today's deluge.'

'And I wasn't aware we were discussing the state of the creeks ... *today!*'

'Well, they can't rise any higher, the rain's stopped!'

Unexpectedly, Kelly's teeth shone whitely in a wide smile which had Paige catching her breath in a taut throat. 'Go back to the city where you belong, little townie, you're out of your element here,' he advised drily. 'You have absolutely no idea of what you're up against, have you?'

'How could I have? I've never been here before!' she retorted, her pride stung. 'Although that still doesn't give you the right to be so patronising. I've always been led to believe country people were friendly and helpful. So far you've been neither!'

'It only seems that way because you don't like what you've been hearing!' His return was cutting in its contempt. 'We're willing to help those who are prepared to accept good advice based on experience. But as to the rest ... well, we'd rather you stay within the boundaries of your metropolises. It causes us far less work and time lost that way.'

Of all the nerve! Anyone would think that the outback belonged solely to him! 'Well, thank *you* for your kind welcoming words, Mr Sinclair!' Paige rounded on him acidly. 'I must remember to return the compliment some time. If I send you a postcard from Greenvale saying, "Wish you were here," you won't take it literally, will you?'

There was the sound of a muffled expletive and then she was brought up short by a forcefully restraining hand on her arm as she attempted to storm past him down the hallway.

'I meant what I said about the roads tomorrow, you stubborn little fool!' he bit out angrily. 'If you must travel, then go east, back the way you've come. In any other direction you're only asking for trouble. We've been waiting on these waters for weeks now.'

Except for one long furious glare Paige gave no acknowledgment of his warning. Right at the moment she was too incensed with his high-handedness to speak at all. Instead, she jerked her arm free, about-faced, and continued on her way with her head held high. Only the violent slamming of the door to her room after she had entered it gave a true indication as to the force of her feelings. She was so mad she could have repeated the action half a dozen times before her temper would have abated.

Not satisfied with insinuating that she was chasing after Stuart Thornton, he had then proceeded to imply that she was not only stubborn and a nuisance, but slightly on the brainless side as well! Okay, so she wasn't fully aware of the conditions in the area, that was still no reason for him to be so arrogant about it. To sound so unwarrantedly satisfied with the thought that she couldn't make it all the way to Greenvale. It was almost as if he had a private reason of his own for not wanting her to meet Stuart again. A moment's reconsideration was all that was required to discount that idea, however. She just couldn't conceive of any way the Stuart Thornton she had met would have any connection with some unknown stockman from some distant outstation.

When morning came Paige was out of bed early, her first action being to rush across the polished wood floor to the window in order to check what the weather was like. Seconds later she was smiling pleasurably to herself. There, she had known it wasn't going to be raining again today. The only clouds to be seen in the bright azure blue sky were light fluffy ones—definitely not dark stormy ones—and she could see for herself by the steam rising in the street that the climbing sun was already beginning to evaporate the moisture left behind the day before. Kelly Sinclair had been wrong, completely and utterly wrong in his forecast, and when she saw him at breakfast it would give her the utmost satisfaction to tell him so!

But after washing and dressing in dark green slacks and a white sleeveless top, she discovered on entering the small dining room at the rear of the hotel that she was the only one present. Of Kelly Sinclair there was no sign.

'Has—um—Mr Sinclair already left?' she asked as

casually as possible of Andy Johnson when she went
to the office to pay her bill as soon as she had finished
her meal.

'Yes, lass, he went back last night,' he smiled. 'Said he
had a lot to do today and that he wanted an early start.'

'I see,' she nodded, feeling somewhat deflated. She
had been looking forward to pointing out how mis-
taken he'd been. 'It is a lovely day, though, isn't it? It
shouldn't take long for the roads to dry out again in
this weather.'

'Mmm, it will certainly make it easier driving for you.
Kelly said you'd be setting off for Sydney again today.'

Oh, he had, had he? Well, he might just have been
a little premature in his supposition, Paige railed
silently.

'It's a pity you had to come so far before finding out
you couldn't reach Greenvale,' Andy was continuing
in a sympathetic tone. 'In a couple of days they don't
expect us to be able to move around here at all.'

'Because of yesterday's rain?'

He laughed at her disbelieving expression. 'No, because of the prolonged rain they've been having in
Queensland.'

'But that's hundreds of miles away!' she protested.

'Maybe, but apparently that's the way their floodwaters usually come,' he relayed. 'Down from the
channel country into your namesake, the Darling,
which takes them across inland New South Wales to
link up with the Murray on the Victorian border. After
that, it's on through South Australia to Lake Alexan-
drina where they finally empty out into the Southern
Ocean.'

Paige absorbed this quickly, then tipped her head to

one side to enquire intently, 'You've never seen these waters arrive?'

Andy shook his head happily. 'No, this will be a new experience for me too.'

'But Mr Sinclair did say in a *couple* of days you wouldn't be able to move, didn't he?'

'That's right, although ...' He stooped and sent her a suspicious look from beneath thick bushy brows. 'You're not thinking of trying to make it to Greenvale, anyway, are you, lass?'

'Well, it is only another hundred odd miles and it is fine weather today,' she murmured persuasively. 'Surely there's plenty of time for me to get there before these supposed waters arrive, otherwise the whole trip's been wasted.'

'I know it sounds feasible,' he conceded slowly, 'but I still don't think Kelly would be very happy if I didn't warn you strongly against it.'

It was enough to send Paige's temper skyrocketing. So, who cared if Kelly Sinclair was happy or not? It was no concern of his whatsoever where she went. She had only asked him for information on the state of the roads, not his permission to use them! But she would show him! They used Volkswagens in cross-country motor rallies, didn't they? They certainly didn't restrict themselves to four-wheel-drive vehicles.

Concealing her anger carefully, she gave a fair imitation of a rueful shrug. 'In that case, it doesn't look as if I have much choice, does it?' she smiled. 'Perhaps I'll have better luck another time.'

'I hope so, lass, I hope so,' Andy smiled back, obviously relieved by her apparent acceptance of the inevitable. 'It can't be very pleasant to have come so far, only to be turned back within sight of your destination, as it were.'

'No. No, it isn't,' she concurred wholeheartedly.

Presently, her single case stowed in the car, Paige bade the hotel's friendly proprietor goodbye and headed down the street to the service station in order to fill the V.W.'s tank with petrol. It was fortunate she had enquired general directions to Greenvale yesterday or else Andy might have become suspicious. As it was, it would be a complete surprise to everyone when she arrived. She might even send that postcard to Mr Sinclair after all, she mused, grinning to herself as she pictured the expression on his face when he received it.

Two miles out of town she turned off the main road and began following what she guessed to be the tracks made by Kelly Sinclair's Land Cruiser the night before. It made the going much more comfortable by not having to pick her own route around all the rocks and holes which lay in wait for the unprepared and, after an hour's concentrated driving, she came to the grudging conclusion that the route had been chosen well. If nothing else, Kelly Sinclair was obviously very familiar with this particular track.

There were a couple of occasions which caused her some concern, all the same—once, when she was too busy watching the fascinating scenery to notice he had given a wide berth to a particular rough section strewn with boulders, and another time when the road had dipped into a causeway and she had found herself staring, alarmed, at the water rushing across it. She had stopped then to test the depth by wading through it barefoot with her slacks pulled above her knees, but to her relief it had only proved to be a foot or so high and by slow steady driving she had managed to ford it without too much difficulty.

The plain she was on now stretched flat and seemingly almost denuded of vegetation except for clumps of spinifex and saltbush to the far horizon, and giving Paige the strangest feeling of being the only person left alive on earth. It was daunting, and more than a little frightening, to imagine being stranded in such an empty and isolated region and, pushing her foot down on the accelerator as hard as she dared, she had her little car speeding along at a pace she had no doubt Kelly Sinclair would describe as being foolhardy.

Her thankful sigh on eventually reaching the trees and sandstone outcrops on the far side was short-lived, however, for as she faithfully followed the Land Cruiser's tracks she found herself heading directly towards the most ominous storm clouds she had ever seen. Black as night, they spread out before her, their billowing formations appearing like some malevolent spirit waiting to devour her in their watery maws. There was no gradual entry into it either. The full torrent hit her windscreen as if she had driven into a waterfall, and as she peered between her flashing wipers Paige's consternation grew. Not only were Kelly's tracks disappearing before her very eyes but the outline of the road was being washed out too! It was merging back into the landscape as if it had never been and leaving her with absolutely nothing at all to follow.

To avoid travelling too far from where the road had last been she came to a rapid halt and prepared to patiently wait out the storm. With luck it wouldn't last for too long and then she could be on her way again.

The only trouble was that after close on ninety minutes of saturating rain, her car wheels spun helplessly in the resultant mire as soon as she attempted to start off again, and it didn't take long to conclude that there was no way in the world it was going to move from where it was without more help than she was able to give it.

In dismay she swept worried eyes around the once again sun-drenched horizon, fighting determinedly against a rising panic at being afoot in such inhospitable terrain. At least she wouldn't die of thirst, she attempted to smile wryly, for the gently sloping creek bed she had crossed just prior to the storm's arrival was now a gurgling waterway rushing pell-mell into the distance. And if she stayed by the car, which was a distinctive bright red, then it possibly wouldn't be long before her plight was discovered. The worst thing she could do would be to wander away seeking help on her own, especially since she had no idea in which direction her nearest help lay.

There was a rocky mound a few hundred yards away, though, and deciding it would give her a better vantage point from which to survey her surrounds Paige struck out for it at a brisk pace. Almost to its base she thought she detected a movement from the corner of her eye and swung around hurriedly, straining to pinpoint what had attracted her attention. The steaming heat haze didn't help her efforts at all and, finally giving up after some long frowning minutes, she was preparing to walk on when it happened again. This time, however, it seemed a little closer and over a wider area. Could it be a mob of sheep? she wondered. If it was then perhaps help was nearer at hand than she had at first believed. A tremor, half relief and half excitement, raced through her and she began running the last few steps to the mound in order to gain elevation and a clearer view.

Scrambling over the crumbling rocks, she paused and looked outwards again. Yes, it was definitely closer, although she still couldn't quite distinguish just what it was. Low to the ground and faintly reddish brown in colour, through the dancing shifting mirage it appeared to Paige like a large herd of sheep churning up dust, except that there wasn't any dust after the rain, and here and there in the midst of it a diamond glint would suddenly sparkle brightly and then disappear. But sheep wouldn't glint, she grimaced. Nor did she think they moved quite as rapidly as this was doing.

Abruptly she drew in a sharp breath, a coil of nervous apprehension tightening in the pit of her stomach. Sheep might not glint ... but *water* did! Fed by two days of storms the floodwaters were pouring down any avenue they could find, and she stared, momentarily mesmerised, as they suddenly burst across her line of vision. A frothing wave searched out a path for the great mass which was following down the already half filled creek she had crossed so recently, and finding the banks too low to contain its gushing force surged over the land on either side to leave behind an inland sea where moments before there had been rocks and earth and scrub.

Her spell broken as she realised the danger, Paige clambered swiftly to the highest point of the eroded ridge and gazed helplessly back at her car. Oh, please, she prayed inwardly, please don't let it be swept away! It had all her money, her clothes, everything except what she stood up in, inside it. But the swollen stream paid no mind to her voiceless pleas as it engulfed the small vehicle in a rapacious maelstrom and, floating it effortlessly back into the main channel, submerged it completely beneath the heaving waters as they continued on their destructive way.

Now what was she to do? Paige despaired, hugging her arms about her midriff. The water which had rushed to meet the base of her haven didn't look to be particularly deep, she guessed about two to three feet, but it was an effective gaoler for all that. Together with the fair sized plateau a short distance to her left there was similar such islands dotted spasmodically towards the horizon, but even if she could make it to one of them, was there much point in merely exchanging one prison for another? Her only hope now appeared to be in signalling a plane overhead. One of the emergency service's craft, perhaps, checking on isolated homesteads and the like. Otherwise . . .? She sank down on to a wind-smoothed rock and her forehead drooped forward to rest on her updrawn knees. She really didn't fancy considering 'otherwise'!

How long she stayed in that position Paige had no idea, but when she lifted her head again her shadowy silhouette was being cast considerably further over the rippling water and she shivered at the thought of having to spend the night in such uninviting circumstances. Idly, she combed her fingers through her curling russet hair and began to gather a handful of stones. Even throwing those into the water one by one was better than doing nothing. She pulled her hand back, preparing to hurl the first one, and then stopped, blinked, and blinked again, her little missiles falling unheeded to the ground as she leapt to her feet and began waving her arms furiously above her head. There was someone out there! Someone on a horse. She was going to make it to Greenvale after all!—she almost danced in her thankfulness.

It took quite some time for the solitary rider to reach her, but long before he did most of Paige's grateful anticipation had been replaced by shaky trepidation. Her rescuer was none other than her unhelpful informant of the night before—Kelly Sinclair—and as he came closer it was all too apparent what he felt about finding her in such a predicament. His eyes were steel-hard and coloured to match, not a scrap of blue in evidence. His mouth was set in forbidding lines—no touch of humour there now, she noted tremulously—and there was such an aura of barely leashed tension about him that she couldn't meet his stabbing gaze but kept her bright head slightly lowered as she chewed at a soft underlip.

'Of all the self-willed, ignorant, senseless, stupid idiots, you would have to be the worst!' he flayed her unmercifully in a tone of scathing contempt. 'It would be no more than your just deserts if I damned well left you where you are!'

The knowledge that she couldn't honestly refute any of his indictments had Paige bowing her head even lower beneath his wrath and whispering, 'I'm sorry,' in a deeply contrite and subdued voice.

'You're sorry!' he mimicked with a short mirthless laugh, unimpressed. 'Nowhere near as sorry as you will be by the time your protracted visit's over, I'll guarantee. I just hope the perverse determination which brought you out here today, against all advice to the contrary, is sufficient to sustain you during your enforced stay!'

'What do you mean ... enforced stay?' she queried warily, her brows drawing together in a frown.

'Exactly what I said,' he retorted. 'Having forced your way in here, you're not going to find it so easy to get out again, Miss Darling. When it floods in the outback it's not for a few days, it's for *weeks*! By the look of this,' he turned slightly in the saddle to survey the water surrounding them with a sardonic smile, 'I should say you can expect to still be here in five or six weeks' time.'

'But that's impossible!' Paige stared at him appalled. 'I can't be away for that long!'

'The decision isn't yours to make any more. You forfeited your opportunity to do that when you drove north instead of east from Tingala this morning.'

'But I ...'

'Forget the "buts", Miss Darling,' he interrupted her coldly. 'Only I wouldn't suggest you stay up on that ridge for too much longer, otherwise we might both end up being stranded here. These waters *are* still rising, you know.'

As if to add weight to his words his mount, which had been standing quietly until now, began to show signs of restlessness, as if anxious to be on the move again.

'Where—where shall I sit?' she questioned doubtfully after slithering down the incline and coming to rest just above the water line.

'Up here,' Kelly nodded briefly to a spot directly in front of him.

Paige started chewing at her lip again. The prospect

of sitting in such close contact was more than a little discouraging. 'Couldn't I sit behind you instead?' she suggested tentatively.

His expression temporarily became wry, as if he knew exactly what was going through her mind. 'I think you'd find it somewhat uncomfortable if you tried. Mercury has a tendency to buck with a pillion on his rump.'

'Oh, I see.' Innocent green eyes were ingenuously raised. 'You find it hard to control him, do you?'

'Not particularly. I just can't imagine you remaining seated while I did so, that's all,' he drawled.

Now it was Paige's mien which turned wry. He had a point there, she reluctantly conceded. One heave from that sinewy creature and she had a fair idea of exactly where she would be heading. But when it became obvious Kelly had no intention of making it easier for her to mount by bringing the horse closer, she sent him one sparkling glare of resentment and ploughed angrily through the water towards them.

'Where's your car?' he asked a few minutes later when she was seated stiffly before him and he had heeled Mercury into movement.

She nodded glumly in the general direction of the creek. 'In there somewhere.'

'Serves you right!'

The callous beast! Tears welled into her eyes which she immediately wiped away with a surreptitious hand. Even if it was her own fault there was no need for him to be so unfeeling about it. She had scrimped and saved for years to buy that vehicle.

'I hope it was insured,' he added.

'Oh, I just bet you do!' she flashed at him sarcastically. 'I'm sure nothing would give you greater pleasure than to hear me say it wasn't!'

'Well, was it?'

'No, damn you, it wasn't!' Her lips trembled uncontrollably. 'N-not for this type of accident, anyway.'

A heavily expelled breath and he recommended, 'Maybe next time you'll listen when somebody gives you advice on matters you know nothing about.'

'And maybe next time I'll be lucky enough to ask someone who gives better advice too!' she gibed over one shoulder. 'You said the floodwaters wouldn't be here for another couple of days and that I only needed a four-wheel-drive.'

'And so you did ... to reach Greenvale.'

'Well, what else do you think I'm out here for, if its *not* to reach Greenvale?' she demanded, exasperated.

'That's what I've been trying to work out,' he divulged drily. 'You see, this happens to be part of Bindaburra. The turn-off for Greenvale is about five miles on the other side of the Barren Plains.'

Oh, no! She had been so busy congratulating herself on how easy it was following in his tracks that it had never occurred to her that she might be on the wrong road.

'You mean ...' She swallowed hard and started again. 'You mean, we aren't anywhere near the Thornton's property?'

'Not in terms of your reckoning,' he smiled suddenly. 'They're neighbours, but about fifty miles in that direction,' indicating to their right.

'And it won't be flooded there yet?' Paige queried, unsure whether it was that unexpected smile or anticipation of his answer that was making her so breathless.

Kelly shook his head slowly, implicitly. 'Not yet.'

With her shoulders visibly slumping Paige turned to stare out unseeingly over Mercury's dark head. Her parents had always warned her she would come to rue her impulsiveness one day. How much she would regret it they couldn't possibly have suspected!

Of necessity their pace wasn't a very fast one, a walk most often but occasionally a canter, and after an hour's unaccustomed riding Paige found herself becoming stiff and sore.

'Are we likely to arrive at wherever we're going today?' she sniped, brushing a fly away from her face irritably.

'Why, would you have preferred to stay where you were?' he countered just as satirically.

She gave an involuntary shudder and then sighed. In a situation like this any company was better than none at all.

'I'm sorry, but it really hasn't been one of my better days,' she attempted to make a joke of it, but it had a hollow sound impossible to disguise and she hurried on to enquire, '*Is* it much farther?'

'Not very,' he advised. 'Near that stand of trees up ahead.'

Paige peered forward, eyes squinting against the glare of the lowering sun, her lips pulling into a grimace of disbelief. Just up ahead! It looked miles away to her. She could only just make it out! And the fact that it was so far from where he'd found her set her thinking.

'Were you working near the creek?' she puzzled. 'Is that how you came across me so quickly?'

'Mmm, I drove some cattle up on to the plateau this

morning. After the rain there'll be feed up there to keep them going for a few weeks.'

'And is that where you saw me from?'

'Uh-huh!' A brief pause and he went on mockingly, 'What were you trying to do, set a record for the plains crossing? It's lucky you didn't have a breakdown in the middle of them, the way you were driving.'

She didn't bother to explain why she had been travelling so fast. It was doubtful he would appreciate, or condone, her reason. Besides, knowing he had seen her that early in the day provoked more important thoughts and she swung around quickly to voice them, wincing as her suffering muscles protested against the action.

'You didn't by any chance also happen to see me become bogged, did you?' she probed suspiciously.

There was no admission on his part, merely the ironic observation, 'I'm amazed you didn't realise that's what would happen when you stopped in that downpour.'

'Well, what else could I do?' she flared. 'The rain was washing out your tracks and I thought stopping was better than wandering all over the countryside getting hopelessly lost.'

The blue of his eyes was very much to the fore now and, to Paige's chagrin, bright with amusement. 'You were following in my tracks?'

'Yes,' she owned reluctantly, flushing, and dropping her gaze.

'But you knew I wasn't going to Greenvale!'

'I didn't intend to miss the turn-off. It—it just happened, that's all.'

'Because you were too occupied with the idea of

proving me wrong for having told you not to attempt the journey?'

It was too near the truth for her liking and she shied away from it, discomfited. 'At least *I* didn't leave anyone stranded without going to their aid!' she gibed defensively. 'I could have drowned for all you cared. And if I hadn't walked across to that ridge when I did, I probably would have done.'

'But you did walk across there and I knew that's where you were headed,' she was informed in a cooling tone.

'You still could have made some effort to help with my car,' she sniffed reproachfully.

'There wasn't time.'

'And I suppose it was because you had just too much to do that you left me sitting there all afternoon, worrying myself sick thinking about what might happen if I wasn't rescued!' she retorted.

'Of course you would have been rescued!' he countered, contemptuous of her fears. 'When you failed to arrive at Greenvale they would have immediately ...' Halting abruptly, he stared down at her, incredulity written all over his face. 'Good God! You didn't get Andy to radio the Thorntons and let them know you were on your way, did you? In fact, beside myself, no one else has a clue as to where you might be at the moment, have they?' And without waiting for a reply he continued witheringly, 'Hell! How could anyone be that blindly stupid? I should have done what I first considered doing, after all!'

'Which was?' Paige questioned, flippantly arching her brows in order to conceal her lacerated pride.

'To bloody well leave you on that ridge overnight!

A few more hours spent pondering your reckless actions might have done you the world of good,' he grated harshly.

'Only "might"?' she made herself mock.

He nodded decisively. 'With someone as contrary as you, Miss Darling, nothing could possibly be a certainty!' he disparaged.

CHAPTER TWO

At long last they arrived at their destination, and Paige sighed thankfully as Mercury finally carried them out of the water and on to relatively dry land again at the foot of a tree- and scrub-covered rise. After Kelly's last derisive remark there had been a stony silence between them for the remainder of the journey and she was looking forward to the chance of escaping his censorious company. Only too aware of her own foolishness, she didn't need him rubbing it in at every opportunity!

Coming out from between the trees a small wooden house stood directly in their path, surrounded by some dilapidated outbuildings, and it was to this that Kelly guided them.

Paige looked about her with a frown, unable to refrain from asking, 'Is *this* Bindaburra?'

'That's right,' came the indifferent answer as he swung to the ground and tied Mercury's reins to a post in the slip-rail fence. 'Home sweet home until we can use the Land Cruiser to get across to Ainslie.'

'Ainslie?' she echoed, bewildered.

'The head station,' laconically.

Prickles of realisation began to creep down her spine and her dark-lashed eyes widened in dismay. 'Are you telling me that we're the only two here? That this,' she grimaced and pointed to the house and its few associated buildings, 'is all that Bindaburra consists of?'

'Not quite.' One corner of his mouth tilted obliquely. 'There's approximately a hundred and fifty thousand acres that goes with it.'

'Oh, very droll!' she applauded sarcastically. 'But that wasn't what I was meaning. I thought ...'

'That you were being taken to some gracious homestead where you could enjoy a life of ease while you were waiting for the waters to recede?' he inserted disdainfully. 'Well, no such luck, I'm afraid, Miss Darling! But I shouldn't complain too much if I were you, it could have been worse. At least this place was originally built as a homestead and not a boundary rider's hut. The equipment's still here to generate our own electricity.'

'Well, isn't that a blessing!' she mocked. 'But for your information, I was not envisaging a life of ease, I just thought there would be more people here,' thereby enabling her to avoid contact with him as much as possible.

'Sorry, but you'll just have to make do with my company for a while. Unless, of course,' he surveyed her drily, 'you're planning to stay up there for the duration.'

Paige wrinkled her dainty nose explicitly and made a move to dismount, stopping with a suppressed groan after her first half-hearted attempt. 'I can't,' she declared flatly. 'I'm too stiff to move anywhere at the moment.'

'By that, I gather you're not used to riding,' Kelly grinned, much to her annoyance, as he stepped forward to grasp her firmly about the waist and lift her to the ground.

'Whatever gave you that idea?' she quipped facetiously, grateful to be back on her own two feet again, even if she did feel incapable of walking. 'I always ride my tried and trusty steed to and from work in the city every day. Didn't you know? It's the only way to travel on a crowded highway.'

His eyes slid over her consideringly. 'You're a sarcastic little devil,' he eventually revealed his inner musings. 'But at least it should prevent our sojourn here from becoming dull.'

A point in her favour! Paige could hardly credit it. Although she didn't have time to dwell on it either, because he was obviously waiting for her to accompany him to the house and it took all her concentrated efforts to reach the verandah without vocally complaining at every step she was forced to take.

The house was clean but spartan inside, with only the barest of essentials having been installed. Three rooms showed signs of habitation—the old-fashioned bathroom, the dining room which had been converted into a makeshift bedroom, and the large kitchen which was able to accommodate a table and chairs with ease. The remainder of the rooms appeared, in the main, to have been taken over as storerooms and contained a variety of items the like of most of which Paige had never seen before.

'Well, that's about it,' Kelly shrugged indolently when they returned to the kitchen. 'Make yourself at home and I'll finish what needs doing outside before it starts getting dark.'

Paige nodded uncertainly and watched him leave with some misgivings. Make herself at home doing what? She had nothing of her own with her and she didn't care to go poking inquisitively around someone else's house, especially when every step was bordering on agony. Perhaps she could have a bath, she mused, her lips pursing thoughtfully. It might help to relieve some of her aches and pains, although what she was going to do for clean clothes afterwards she had no idea. Maybe she would have to go searching through some of the cupboards after all to see if she could find a spare blanket, or sheet, or something similar, in which to swathe herself so that she could wash out her clothes and let them dry overnight ready for tomorrow.

In time, she managed to find some sheets—half a dozen in assorted colours and patterns, to her surprise— as well as some towels in a cupboard in one of the storerooms, and deciding on a bronze and lemon striped sheet and a bright orange towel she headed for the bathroom with a smile of anticipation lighting her face.

Ah, bliss! she sighed a few minutes later as she slid further down into the steaming water, closing her eyes in contentment. It was just what the doctor ordered and she was certain she could feel it doing her protesting limbs good already.

The sound of the door being swung open and the

rather short-tempered exclamation, 'I wondered where the hell you'd disappeared to!' completely demolished her sense of wellbeing, however, and her eyes flew wide open again, righteously indignant, while she dragged her knees up to her chest and wrapped her arms protectively around them in a flurry of splashing.

'Well, now you know, would you mind getting out!' she blazed, the colour of her cheeks deepening noticeably under his unabashed appraisal. 'Just in case you haven't become aware of it yet, I'm trying to have a bath and I would prefer it in private!'

Kelly shrugged impassively and turned for the hall. 'I know what you need,' he drawled enigmatically on his way out.

Paige was left staring at the empty doorway, perplexed, and not a little apprehensive. 'I don't need anything!' she shouted after him.

'Not much you don't,' he retorted a short while later when he reappeared in the opening and walked unhesitatingly towards the bath with a plastic bag of white crystals in one hand and a bottle of brown liquid in the other. 'Soda and vinegar to ease those aching muscles,' he explained drily as he calmly poured a liberal amount of each into the water, much to her embarrassment.

'Thank you,' she muttered grudgingly from between clenched teeth, not looking at him. '*Now* may I please have some privacy?'

'Surely,' he agreed, laughter uppermost in his voice. 'There's really no cause for you to look quite so mortified, though. Once he's been married for a while a man becomes quite accustomed to seeing a woman in various stages of undress.'

Which was no consolation to Paige, seeing she wasn't his wife, but once the door had been shut she could relax again—bodily, even if not mentally. So he was married, was he? It didn't really surprise her, even though it had given her a moment of unaccountable depression when he'd mentioned it. She could imagine him being very appealing to the opposite sex—when he wasn't being unmercifully denigrating, that was!—what with his rugged good looks and that element of essential maleness about him.

She began to soap herself slowly, meditatively. But where was his wife? Back at ... what had he called it? ... Ainslie? It would hardly be much of a marriage, would it, with them living on separate properties and only seeing each other when he returned to the head station? Or perhaps he didn't always work on Binda-burra, perhaps he was only here temporarily. Yesterday evening he had said, '*While* I'm working on Binda-burra ...' Mmm, that would make more sense, she decided. He was probably filling in for someone else at the moment and that was why his wife wasn't with him.

By the time she had finished her bath, washed her hair—she had figured she might as well when the shoulder-length ends had become wet through having nothing suitable to tie it back with—and then showered herself off, Paige was feeling distinctly less stiff and after rubbing herself briskly dry she set about form-ing the sheet into a secure covering.

Without fasteners of any kind this proved a little difficult to accomplish, but after several frustrating efforts she felt it was wrapped safely enough around her and she quickly washed out her own clothes in the basin. There was a comb on the shelf next to the bath, which she didn't think Kelly would mind if she used and then, draping her wet outfit over one arm and picking up her still damp shoes with the other, she made her way to the back verandah where she had previously noticed a pair of jeans hanging on a temporary line. Neatly pegging her clothes alongside them, she placed her shoes as near to the edge of the verandah as possible so that they might catch the early morning sun, and then stood pensively by the rail for a few moments looking past the fenced yard where Mercury was picking desultorily at the grass to the flooded land beyond.

'Regretting it isn't Stuart who's marooned here with you?'

The heavily sardonic question caught Paige by surprise. Nothing had been further from her mind in actual fact. She had merely been appreciating the hushed tranquillity and majestic scope of the scene spread before her as the waters began to reflect a blood-red hue from the scarlet orb of the sun as it sank closer and closer towards the distant horizon. For some inexplicable reason, however, she was reluctant to confess it had been the strange hard beauty of her surroundings and not Stuart's absence which had caused her thoughtfulness and, in consequence, her reply was flippantly, although not altogether truthfully, given.

'Naturally!' She made it sound unbelievable he should even have begun to contemplate otherwise. 'After all, he was the one I travelled all this way to see, and I'm sure *his* attitude would have been far less disparaging than yours. He realises not everyone's perfect and that some of us do, occasionally, fall short of your lofty expectations and make regrettable errors of judgment!'

'Except that in your case it wasn't an error of judgment ... but of temperament!' Kelly was quick to retort with stinging emphasis. 'Like a lot of others of your sex, you mistakenly believe a beguiling face makes you a law unto yourselves and entitles you to do exactly as you please, regardless of the trouble or inconvenience you cause others in the process!'

Paige drew in a sharply resentful breath. 'I do no such thing!' she protested, eyes flashing angrily. 'And how you could possibly make such a dogmatic statement, I don't know! Two limited meetings is hardly sufficient for anyone to gauge another's character.'

'Oh, I wouldn't say that.' His lip curled scornfully. 'Your remark of a moment ago was quite explicit, I thought, and I've certainly seen your type often enough before. Every year they arrive in their droves for the annual races and ball, the same as you, and every year their seasons are the same. They're hoping to hook some eligible bachelor—with as large an acreage as possible, of course—and thus provide themselves with immediate entry into the ranks of the squatocracy!'

It was obvious denial would be useless and so she chose to defend her false position as best she could by declaring, 'There's nothing wrong in wanting to improve one's lot in life, Mr Sinclair, and if some of these eligible bachelors have been hooked, as you describe it, then I daresay they were quite willing to have it that way. Even in the outback it *is* still the man who does the proposing, isn't it?'

'In other words, the end justifies the means as far as you're concerned, is that it?'

She shrugged indifferently. 'Sometimes, although I

don't know why you should feel so strongly about it.' A long taunting look reached out to him from beneath curling lashes. 'It wouldn't by any chance have anything to do with that disagreeable emotion, envy, would it?'

His short bark of laughter was completely without humour. 'No, Miss Darling, it would not!' he snapped incisively. 'Disgust would be a better description for what I feel towards your kind of calculating female.'

Her kind of . . . ! Paige's eyes glittered furiously as she stormed closer to where he stood by the steps, long fingers resting lightly on lean hips. After what she had been through today she was in no mood to listen to his unfounded judgment of her actions.

'Is that so?' she gibed acidly. 'Well, let me tell you something too, Kelly Sinclair! You're not the only one who feels distaste round here, because your sanctimonious, holier-than-thou attitude doesn't exactly turn me on either! So I did come for the races, and I did try to reach Greenvale when I shouldn't have, so what business is it of yours? Who in blazes do you think you are, anyway? The self-appointed guardian of the inland?'

'No, just someone who sees you for what you really are. A brazen little opportunist who wasn't going to let something as unimportant as a flood put a halt to her avaricious schemes!'

'H-how dare you!'

Paige was too wrathfully indignant to even get the words out clearly, but the action she accompanied them with was certainly concise enough. A hand was sent flying towards his tanned face with all the force she could put behind it.

Unfortunately, what she hadn't allowed for was the

fact that in her desire to make sure her blow connected she had moved too close, and as he threw up his left arm to block her attack the back of his hand clipped her under the chin and sent her staggering backwards. Unable to regain her balance owing to the hampering folds of the sheet, she collided with one of the verandah roof supports and fell awkwardly, cracking her cheek-bone against the rail on the way down with a force that brought involuntary tears rushing into her eyes.

'Hell, I'm sorry! Are you okay?' Kelly sank lithely down on to his haunches beside her, a worried frown furrowing his forehead.

With a hand held to her throbbing cheek Paige cast him a watery look of accusation. 'No, I'm not! I feel like I've been kicked by a mule,' she grumbled plaintively. 'What were you trying to do, disfigure me for life?'

'Stop exaggerating,' he recommended wryly. 'It was an accident and you know it.'

'No, I don't,' she perversely refused to admit the truth. 'For all I know you might be one of those men who get a kick out of knocking women around.'

His eyes were very blue and very provoking as they gazed directly into hers. 'Then perhaps you'd better think twice before ever attempting the same again, hmm?'

Paige looked away, suddenly uncomfortable, but uncertain whether her discomfiture was caused by his words or his expression. 'Well, you had no right to say I was avaricious and an opportunist,' she complained sulkily.

'If the cap fits . . .' Broad shoulders lifted implicitly.

'Oh, go away and leave me alone, I've had just about as much as I can take of your know-it-all opinions!'

She shook her head despairingly and brushed the finger-tips of her free hand across her increasingly wet lashes. 'So far today I've lost my car, my clothes, and my money; come close to being drowned; been made to sit on the iron-hard back of a horse for God knows how many miles until it was agony to move; and then had my head thumped around so it feels like a football! And—and all you can think to do while this is going on is to make derogatory remarks and c-call me n-names!' she hiccuped mournfully.

Kelly's lips twisted into a rueful grin and then he had scooped her into his arms and risen smoothly to his feet before Paige could utter a word of protest.

'Come on, Rusty, what you need is a cup of tea, a couple of aspirins, and something to eat. I don't suppose you've had any food since breakfast, have you?' He quirked one brow upwards questioningly.

'My lunch was in the car,' she sighed, the strong sense of security his supporting arms gave her completely overcoming any thought of objection to his action. Although not his use of a nickname as she pointed out succinctly, 'My name isn't Rusty, it's Paige, thank you!'

'Pity,' he smiled down at her unrepentantly. 'Rusty seems to suit you.'

'Only in your opinion, Mr Sinclair, not in mine.'

'Kelly,' he corrected lazily.

'All right ... Kelly,' she agreed, but promptly added, 'My answer's still the same, though.'

After lowering her on to one of the kitchen chairs he started filling the kettle and bypassing the electric stove, to Paige's surprise, he elected to use the old fuel one instead.

'Doesn't the electric stove work?' she asked as he

passed her on his way to a cupboard at the other end of the room.

'As far as I know it does,' he shrugged.

'You just prefer this one?'

'I guess you could say that,' he nodded, returning to the table with a bottle and some cotton wool. 'They're what I was brought up with, and as most outstations don't have electric stoves then I figure there's not much point in learning different methods.'

Paige could see the logic behind his thinking, but before she could voice any more questions he had spanned her chin with a capable hand and was tilting her face up to the light.

A minute's inspection of her already swelling cheek and she slanted him an enquiring look. 'Well?'

Briefly, a wry grin appeared and then it was gone. 'I'm sorry we haven't any ice but, with luck, this will help,' he replied, releasing her and, unscrewing the cap on the bottle, tipped some of the contents on to the cotton wool.

'That didn't sound very encour ...' She stopped, and sniffed experimentally. 'I know the smell, but I can't put a name to it,' she puzzled.

'Witch-hazel. It's an old remedy for bruises.'

'Oh!' She relaxed slightly and allowed him to continue applying the solution carefully to the painful area. Then she remembered that first enigmatic expression and she sought his face suspiciously. 'Am I going to have a black eye?'

''Fraid so, at least partially,' he drawled, recapping the bottle and disposing of the cotton wool in the flames of the stove.

'And you think that's amusing, don't you?' She

glared resentfully at his back as he began making the tea, and without waiting for him to answer—even if that had been his intention, which she doubted— went on to gibe, 'If you're as callous and unsympathetic as this at home I can't imagine your wife missing you in the slightest when you have to work on an outstation for a while. I think you must have spent too much time on your own. You've forgotten—if you ever cared —that the rest of us have such things as feelings!'

The teapot was placed on the table with a notice-able thump. 'A considered opinion of *yours* this time?' He eyed her satirically.

'Yes!' She wasn't going to back down now.

'Then it will no doubt assuage your compassionate instincts to know that I considerately gave my wife a divorce over four years ago and that, today, she is as happily enjoying her freedom from me as I am mine from her!' he divulged in a rasping tone, the cups and saucers clattering to their resting places this time.

Paige nervously caught at her bottom lip with even white teeth. She certainly couldn't complain about a lack of feeling when he'd imparted that information.

'I'm sorry.' She hunched one shoulder uncomfort-ably. 'Had—had you been married long?'

'Long enough to become disenchanted!'

With marriage in particular, or females in general? she wondered. To relieve the tension she could sense was steadily increasing she tried changing the subject.

'And have you—er—always worked around here?'

'No, not always.' His answer was offered in the most uninformative of voices. 'Why?'

Momentarily she stared back at him, nonplussed, and then her own temper began to reassert itself. 'Because if we're going to be stuck here together for any length of time then we're going to have to talk about *something*!' she fired. 'Or were you just planning to pretend I didn't exist?'

The eyes which raked over her so sharply had reverted to pure grey. 'It's a tempting thought, I admit, but unfortunately I've never been one to indulge in wishful thinking!'

'Oh, what a pity! You must be very disappointed,' she commiserated mockingly. 'Maybe you could lock me in one of the spare rooms instead. That would be almost as good as not having me here, wouldn't it?'

'Nothing could be that good!'

'For me either,' she whispered huskily, hurt by his attitude more than she should have been, and certainly more than she liked, but strangely unable to sustain her anger.

Across the table Kelly was left with only a view of the crown of her head and the sooty smudges of her dark lashes as she lowered her gaze.

'Here, drink this,' he sighed heavily, edging a cup of tea towards her and tossing a packet of aspirins after it. 'A couple of those probably won't go amiss either.'

'Thank you.' Paige accepted them both without lifting her head.

'Would you like one of these as well?'

She had no choice but to look up now and found him holding out a cigarette packet. 'Thank you,' she murmured again, grateful for anything which might help to soothe her frayed nerves.

There was only one thing wrong, her hand was too shaky to hold the cigarette still long enough for him to set a light to it, and in the end he took it back from her, lit it himself, then handed it across again—all without a single comment.

'I'm sorry,' she apologised dejectedly.

'For what?' His brows peaked eloquently.

One smooth-skinned shoulder rose slightly above her covering sheet. She had meant for not being capable of lighting her own cigarette, but now found herself saying, 'For everything, I guess. For not taking your advice, for causing you extra work, for being here, for asking questions you don't want to answer.'

'You don't think you might have missed anything?' he smiled wryly.

Paige wasn't sure whether he was making fun of her or not, but even if he had been she felt too listless to do anything about it. Perhaps she did need food after all, for that last burst of anger certainly seemed to have drained the last of her energy away.

'Only that I'm sorry for not thanking you properly for rescuing me,' she added a little unsteadily. 'I really wouldn't have liked to have stayed on that ridge all night on my own.'

'You mean, even after all that's happened, *I'm* still the lesser of the two evils?' he teased gently.

It was impossible for her to voice an answer, so she made do with a quick nod of her head as an alternative.

'Do you reckon you can hang on till I've cooked some dinner?' It wasn't until a lean hand turned her face up to his that Paige realised he had moved to her side of the table.

'I don't know what you mean,' she frowned.

'I mean the effects of today's events are only now beginning to catch up with you, en masse, and to put it bluntly, you look about bushed.'

'You could be right,' she half smiled faintly. 'I do feel unusually lifeless.'

'Well, if it helps any, ask whatever questions you like,' he invited, relenting.

For a time Paige was too occupied watching him moving about as he prepared dinner to even consider accepting his offer. She supposed men who lived on their own, and especially in circumstances such as these, had to be self-sufficient, but she really hadn't anticipated such smooth efficiency all the same. After seeing her father, whose limits were stretched to make a pot of tea, this was something of a revelation. Nevertheless, her perturbing interest in the man himself, as well as her surroundings, couldn't be denied altogether and eventually she could ignore it no longer.

'How long have you been stationed on Bindaburra, Kelly?' she asked tentatively.

'Only a few weeks,' he replied, not stopping what he was doing. 'It's a new purchase.'

'Oh, what happened to the previous owners?'

'They couldn't make a go of it,' he shrugged. 'Having originally come from near the coast they found the conditions were too different. She didn't like the isolation, he made some bad decisions, the land itself did the rest.'

'The land?'

'Bad seasons,' he elucidated. 'It's usually either boom or bust out here.'

'Not for your boss, though.' If he could afford to buy the property after experiencing the same bad seasons he obviously wasn't short of a dollar! 'Couldn't he have offered them help? Advised them, or something?'

Kelly placed the last of the saucepans on the stove and turned to face her, his expression dry. 'As you should know, advice is only as good as the willingness of the recipient to accept it.'

A deep flush covered Paige's cheeks and she rushed on hastily. 'They didn't listen either?'

'No, Charles kept insisting he knew what he was doing and that he wasn't overstocked. Then, when our rainfall didn't come up to expectations for yet another year, the end result was a foregone conclusion.'

'He lost the lot,' she surmised plausibly.

'That's about it,' he nodded.

'And thereby making it easy for your boss to acquire the place cheaply, I suppose,' she ventured shrewdly.

'Not at all.' His eyes narrowed slightly at the insinuation. 'It was a fair price and Charles was certainly happy with it.'

'But he probably would have been happy just to see the place sold, no matter what the price, wouldn't he?' she persisted.

'Possibly,' he agreed. 'Although that wasn't the case in this instance. What makes you think it might have been?'

She shrugged lightly, uncertain of her reasoning herself. 'Oh, I don't know, just a dislike of monopolies, I guess. You know, the rich get richer and the poor get poorer, sort of thing. Your Mr . . .' Her eyes widened enquiringly. 'What is your boss's name, anyway?'

'Morgan. Bruce Morgan,' he supplied casually.

'Well, your Mr Morgan,' she continued, 'just sounded to me as if he was benefiting at other people's expense.'

Kelly shook his head in disbelief. 'I can't see how. Charles himself put the price on the property and that's what he was paid. There was no haggling. Or are you suggesting he should have been offered more than what was being asked?' He eyed her mockingly.

'No, I suppose not.' Perhaps she had misjudged Bruce Morgan after all. 'But you're very loyal to your boss, aren't you, Kelly?'

After his initial look of surprise, his expression changed to one of amusement. 'Why wouldn't I be? He pays well.'

'And you would prefer to work for him rather than own a property of your own?'

'Sure. Why not?' He turned away to attend to the bubbling saucepans.

The clipped briefness with which his answer had been delivered started Paige wondering whether the question hadn't been put to him on a number of previous occasions. Maybe it had been a bone of contention between him and his wife, she mused. Most women preferred to have their own home rather than having to make do with someone else's. Or perhaps he just couldn't afford to buy one and didn't like having to admit as much. She could imagine that most of them—even somewhat run-down Bindaburra—would cost a great deal to purchase, and certainly more than the average worker could afford to pay. No, she was to decide finally, the ownership of property wasn't the most auspicious line of questioning she could pursue.

'I presume you used to work on Ainslie, then, before your boss bought this property?' she asked next as he headed across the room towards a mini-sized fridge.

'Uh-huh,' he replied absently, opening the door and extracting a plastic container. 'How do you like your steak done?'

The change of topic caught her unprepared and she

stammered, 'Oh—er—medium to well done, please.'

'I can't guarantee that's how it will be, but I'll try,' he grinned.

'As long as it's not still bleeding all over the plate I don't mind,' she smiled back. Knowing herself to be second only to her father as one of the world's worst cooks she wasn't in a position to complain no matter how it turned out. 'So you don't always work on outstations?' she returned to the subject which interested her most.

Kelly dropped two large pieces of meat on to the grill and then slanted her an intent glance over his shoulder. 'You have quite a thirst for knowledge, haven't you?' he drawled.

'I'm sorry,' she apologised immediately, stiffly, although still feeling she was entitled to remind him, 'But you did say I could ask you whatever I liked.'

'That's okay, I wasn't objecting ... just observing,' he informed her wryly. 'I would be interested to learn what prompted your curiosity, though.'

'Well ...' She spread her hands significantly wide. 'This is my first visit to the outback,' and probably her last, she added silently, 'so it's only natural that I would want to find out as much about it as I can while I'm here, isn't it?'

'Mmm, except for one thing.'

'And that is?'

'So far, none of your questions have actually concerned the outback, as such!'

Paige was positive there wasn't an inch of her face which wasn't scarlet and it was impossible to pretend she hadn't realised her questions had been of a more personal nature.

'Oh—er—well, I—I expect that's because I always think the people who live here are as much a part of the outback as the land itself,' she offered selfconsciously after a flustered beginning. 'I mean, it's how the inhabitants live and—and what they do that tells you most about a place, isn't it?'

'And knowing that Bindaburra has only just been added to the boss's holdings, and that I normally work on Ainslie, teaches you something about the area, does it?' he questioned lazily.

'Of course!' She put as much conviction into her tone as she could. 'It tells me ...'

'Mmm?' A dark brow quirked aggravatingly.

'It tells me ...' She tried again but came to a halt at the same point.

'You've already said that.'

'Oh, stop it!' she pleaded anguishedly, suddenly close to tears again. Her brain just wasn't functioning quickly enough at the moment to attempt any sort of feasible evasion. 'Naturally I'm interested in what you do and where you work. I've never met anyone who works on a large station before!'

'Aren't you forgetting Stuart?'

'Not really. From what he had to say about his life out here I gather he prefers just to live on his family's station, not to actually _work_ on it,' she relayed somewhat drily.

'That'd be Stuart,' he acknowledged with a sharp nod. 'Easy come, easy go, that's his motto. It's just as well his brother doesn't feel the same way.'

'Oh, has he got a brother?' she was startled into asking. 'I was under the impression he was an only child.'

'But now that you know he isn't, and especially since Russ is four years his senior, I suppose that would make him a much less attractive proposition for you, wouldn't it?'

'Not at all! I never considered him that in the first place,' she retorted.

The biting return she anticipated didn't eventuate as Kelly turned his attention once more to the sizzling steaks, but she could sense he wasn't convinced by her denial and she stubbed out her cigarette with a dismal sigh.

'Is there something I can do to help?' she asked softly, half rising to her feet. 'Lay the table, or ...'

'No, thanks.' Her offer was curtly refused before it had been fully made. 'Just sit where you are, it won't be long.'

Subsiding on to her seat again, Paige tugged her covering into a more comfortable position, the action jogging her memory. 'I hope you didn't mind me commandeering one of your sheets, but I didn't know what else to use for a change of clothes,' she murmured.

'No worries,' he shrugged indifferently. 'Perhaps you'd better keep it and see if you can't make yourself something to wear from it, as well as a couple of the others that are in the cupboard. There's needles and thread in the drawer over there,' nodding towards the dresser by the window, 'but no sewing machine, I'm afraid.'

'Oh, that doesn't matter,' she exclaimed, unconcerned. She was only too pleased at the thought of having some material to work with. 'It's very good of you to let me cut them up. You're sure your boss won't mind?'

On his way to the table Kelly halted and stared at

her blankly. 'What the hell's he got to do with it?'

'Well, they *are* his property, aren't they? Or—
or do you have to provide your own?'

His mouth curved wryly. 'No, they're store issued.'

'Store issued?'

'The station store. They buy them in bulk lots for
the homestead, the men's quarters, and the outstations.'

'I see,' she nodded thoughtfully. 'Then of course
I'll replace them.'

'Oh, don't be so damned ridiculous!' He ran a hand
irritably around his neck. 'The loss of a few sheets is
hardly likely to set the property's financial stability
tottering, and if you start making offers like that I can
assure you you're going to offend people.'

'In that case, thank you very much,' she smiled hesitantly.

'Right!' He brushed aside her gratitude brusquely.
'Now we've finally got that settled, let's get dinner on
the table.'

The meal, plain but wholesome, was very palatable
and Paige was feeling far more like her normal self by
the time she had finished, even though it had been
eaten in a somewhat strained atmosphere. The incident
concerning the sheets had inexplicably seemed to upset
Kelly and, reluctant to inadvertently aggravate the
situation, she kept silent until they had almost completed the clearing away. Her offer of help not being
refused on this occasion.

'You must find the evenings very long when you're
here on your own,' she eventually remarked in a light
tone, hoping to relieve some of the discord.

'Not so I've noticed.' His reply was disdainfully,
annoyingly, squashing. 'Why, are you afraid that you

will? That you'll become bored without your T.V. and bright city lights to amuse you?'

'No, that hadn't occurred to me!' she glared, exasperated. 'If you must know, I was trying to make conversation, although I realise now that I'm only wasting my time. Maybe I was slow to recognise the obvious, but you can heave a sigh of relief because I've finally made it! Nothing I say or do is going to alter either your opinion or your attitude ... because you just *don't* like me, do you, Kelly?'

'Should I?'

Not having expected him to admit it quite so baldly she could only gaze up at him, shocked, her eyes failing to hide the unaccountable pain his admission caused. 'No, I guess not,' she whispered faintly.

'Well, don't take it so hard,' he counselled drily. 'Not even someone with your looks can expect to go through life with *every* male they meet succumbing to their charms.'

The touch of mocking amusement in his supposition flicked Paige on the raw and her chin lifted defensively. 'Oh, I wasn't upset,' she lied. 'I was just surprised that you should have put it so bluntly. However, there are benefits, because it now gives me the opportunity to say that I don't particularly care much for you either, Kelly Sinclair! You see, the overbearing and egotistical male has never been one of my favourite forms of humanity.'

'The same as self-complacent, ignorant little townies who think they can drive all over the outback as if they were in some city suburb aren't mine?' he enquired with biting softness.

'Exactly!' She allowed herself the satisfaction of an

uncaring smile as she tossed the last of the cutlery into the drawer and pushed it closed. 'But now, if you'll excuse me—and I'm sure you will—I think I'll go for a walk. I feel like a change of air all of a sudden.'

With her hand already turning the door handle, the taunting words, 'Mind you don't get bitten,' floated after her and she turned swiftly, emerald eyes narrowing warily.

'By what?' she probed.

'Who knows?' he shrugged blandly, leaning back against the dresser. 'But we're not the only species to have our routine disturbed by floods, remember.'

In response, Paige raised one of her own shoulders indifferently and continued onwards. He was only trying to make her nervous, she decided with a grimace. Nevertheless, she kept to the verandah as she wandered slowly along, unable to see much at all once she had left the lights of the kitchen behind because the moon was only a thin crescent high in the star-festooned sky above.

At the clothesline she put out a hand to see how her slacks were drying and felt a sharp sting on her neck and then another on her arm which she slapped at angrily. Mosquitoes! Fortunately, her legs were covered, but wherever there was any exposed skin they were attacking voraciously and, swatting frantically as she went, she hurried back to the kitchen as quickly as possible.

Kelly was seated comfortably at the table when she entered, a book held in one hand, a steaming cup of coffee nearby. 'You weren't gone very long, didn't you enjoy your walk?' he looked up to query innocently as she pushed the door shut heavily behind her.

Paige curled her nails into the palms of her hands, as much to stop herself from scratching at the bites as in an attempt to control her feelings. 'I enjoyed it very much, as a matter of fact,' she perjured herself brazenly, while desperately trying to ignore the irritating lumps which were already beginning to dot her skin. 'It was ... very peaceful.'

'No annoying insects?'

'Insects?' She opened her eyes artlessly wide as she edged towards the hallway. 'No, none at all.'

'So where are you heading now?' he asked on noting her anxious movements. 'For another walk, on the inside this time?'

'To the bathroom, actually,' she retorted through clenched teeth. If she didn't put something on those bites soon she would scratch herself to pieces. 'That is, if you have no objections?'

He held out an inviting hand, his expression mocking. 'As I said before, make yourself at home.'

'Thank you,' she gibed sweetly, then fled before he could detain her any longer.

The cold water she applied via a sponge had little effect, however, and in desperation she began rifling through the small cabinet fixed to the wall for a more efficient preparation. When this only proved to contain shaving gear and other such requisites she tried the cold compresses once more—with the same unsuccessful result—and then yielded to the now uncontrollable desire to rake her nails across the reddened inflammations. It was while she was struggling to reach one especially irritating swelling between her shoulder blades that she chanced to see Kelly leaning against the wall watching her lazily.

'You must know that only makes them worse,' he advised ironically.'

'You don't say!' she grimaced caustically, scratching at the back of her hand now. 'But if you think you're going to stand there gloating while I go through purgatory, you've got another think coming!' as she made to slam the door between them.

A booted foot halted its progress halfway and his eyes swept over her flushed features speculatively. 'What makes you think I came to gloat?'

'Didn't you?'

'No, I came to offer this, if you really want to know.' He held up a tube of cream. 'Do you want it or not?'

'Of course I do!' She reached for it eagerly and only just remembered to include a slightly less than gracious, 'Thank you,' before beginning to massage the soothing ointment into her skin.

'If you continue the way you've started, it looks as if the medicine kit is going to be extremely well utilised during your stay,' he commented drily.

Paige halted her ministrations momentarily to cast him a reproachful glare. 'Well, it's not my fault!' she protested. 'I didn't ask to ride that beastly horse for hours, nor to be knocked sideways into the verandah rail. As for these,' her curving mouth pulled into a disgruntled line, 'well, you could have been a little more explicit with your warning, couldn't you?'

'Would it have made any difference?'

'I don't follow you,' she frowned.

He flexed his wide shoulders indolently. 'I figured you would have gone anyway, if only to prove you weren't in need of advice from an overbearing male.'

Would that have been her reaction? Paige wasn't

certain. She had definitely been angry enough at the time to disregard any recommendation he may have given.

'At least I would have been prepared for them,' she accused, not quite able to completely renounce his suggestion. 'I wouldn't have been half eaten alive!'

Dusky blue eyes crinkled disconcertingly. 'I wouldn't bet on that, they're a shrewd and persistent breed out here.'

They weren't the only ones, she noted inwardly, her pulse fluttering.

'Here, your back needs doing as well.' She abruptly found her short reverie broken as she was spun around and her nerveless fingers relieved of the tube she had been holding. 'They did have a field day, didn't they?' he remarked conversationally, brushing her hair forward from her nape, the better to see.

Paige nodded sharply, her fingers fiercely entwined. Too much of her attention was required to discount Kelly's perturbing touch for her to consider speaking. But when she found herself drowsily contemplating what it would be like to have those competent hands sliding over her skin in a more possessive manner, and how it would feel to have that firm mouth covering her own, she was only too willing to hasten into disrupting conversation.

'What—what would happen if something serious happened out here?' she twisted her head briefly to ask. 'Could you contact anyone to let them know?'

'Mmm, there's a portable transceiver in the other room. I usually call in each evening to let the homestead know what's happening.'

'And have you already been in touch with them today?'

'While you were having your bath,' he nodded, re-capping the tube.

Pleased to be able to put a little more distance between them, Paige still couldn't quite meet his gaze as she queried selfconsciously, 'Did you tell them about me?'

Instead of answering her question Kelly countered with a mockingly drawled, 'Why, are you afraid for your reputation?'

'No, not really,' she denied vigorously. 'In circumstances like this I guess it's not uncommon for people to find themselves stranded together, and those who live in the outback would know that better than most. Besides . . .' suddenly she gave a rueful laugh, her soft lips curving, 'I'm sure you've already left no one in any doubt as to what you think of me, or the fact that I'm the last person you would wish to be saddled with for any length of time.'

'A few more smiles like that and I reckon I could become reconciled to it, very easily.'

'But only as long as I did exactly as I was told and didn't open my mouth,' she laughed away his assertion, knowing it wasn't meant to be taken seriously. 'You prefer your women decorative but retiring, don't you, Kelly?'

One well-shaped brow arched tauntingly. 'Another of your considered opinions, Paige Darling?'

She had never met anyone who could place such an unsettling accent on her name before, and goodness knows many had tried, but as on the previous night it was nearly her undoing.

'D-don't tell me I'm wrong, because I—I just won't believe you,' she faltered, an effort needed to keep her smile in place.

'Then I won't attempt to,' he shrugged impassively.

Gradually the glow faded from Paige's eyes, leaving them dark and regretful. She hadn't really intended to goad with her half joking assessment. If anything, it had been meant as a mocking gibe against herself. In some people's eyes she might have qualified for the term decorative, but by no means could she ever have been described as retiring! With a sigh she returned to their original topic of conversation.

'The next time you call the homestead would it be possible to have them send a message for me, please?' she queried diffidently.

'Don't worry, Stuart will already know where you are by now,' he jeered in a harsh voice, his expression condemning as he began striding down the hall.

'I didn't mean Stuart!' she cried, chasing after him.

'Then who...?' He swung around violently, his hands coming to rest on his hips. 'Good God, don't tell me you've got another one dangling on a string back in Sydney as well!'

Paige's chin angled defiantly higher. 'If I have, it's got nothing to do with you!' she flouted. 'But I happen to have been referring to my parents. They'll be worried if they don't hear from me for another couple of weeks.'

'Write down the address and I'll see that word's sent,' he directed curtly.

'Thank you,' she murmured softly, although it was doubtful if he heard her because he was already turning into the kitchen. Paige followed at a more sedate pace.

At the doorway she hesitated, reluctant to disturb him again on seeing he had returned to his book, her thoughts as indecisive as her actions. It seemed the only times he would consent to unbend a little were when she was hurt, she recalled ruefully, but as she had no intention of continually injuring herself in order to bring about a truce then she could visualise her sojourn on Bindaburra being an extremely stormy one. She was also starting to wonder whether it wasn't just herself he didn't like, but women in general. Maybe, as she had considered earlier, his marriage *had* soured him on the whole female race!

Not that it was any concern of hers, of course, and coming to a decision, she determined not to let his unpredictable behaviour ruffle her any further. Not outwardly, anyway. It was intolerable that he had managed to affect her so disastrously this far. Her mind made up, she stepped into the room purposefully.

'If I could borrow a pen and some paper I'll write down that address for you,' she spoke up clearly, unconcerned now whether she disturbed him or not.

Kelly raised his head but only briefly to advise, 'You'll find them in the second drawer over there.'

Paige nodded and went looking. She could be as terse as he was if that was the way he wanted it! On locating a pad and ballpoint pen she leant over the cupboard to note the relevant details, tore off the page, and returned the rest to the drawer.

The written sheet she placed on the table beside his book with a rather tart, 'Thank you!' which he couldn't have avoided hearing this time, then spun on her heels and stalked haughtily out of the room without waiting for any acknowledgment.

Once in the hall she headed for the room where she had discovered the sheets. It was getting late and as there was only one bed visible in the place it seemed as good a time as any to start thinking about where she was going to sleep. If she could find some spare bedding in one of the cupboards she could make up something for herself.

Her first problem turned out to be finding the light switch. The house was in total darkness at that end and after feeling down the door-frame and the adjacent wall, with no result, she ventured carefully into the room in the hopes of locating it on the nearest side wall. One stubbed toe and a cracked shin later she was still no closer to finding it and she glared into the blackness futilely. Where in blazes was it?

The sound of footsteps behind her had Paige whirling towards them, her hip colliding with something sharp on the way which had her suppressing a pained exclamation as a long-suffering voice enquired, 'If it's not a stupid question might I be permitted to ask just what the hell you're doing?'

A sharp indrawn breath to ensure she stayed calm and she replied, 'I wanted to see how many spare blankets there were.'

'In the dark? Wouldn't it be easier if you put the light on?'

'And just what...?' Hurriedly she put a stop to her fiery retort. No, she wasn't going to allow him to deliberately rile her this time. 'I would have done ... if you hadn't hidden the damned switch!' she smouldered.

'It's not hidden,' he imparted blithely, brushing past her, and making Paige wonder how on earth he could see where he was going. 'It's just an old-fashioned ceiling switch, that's all.'

Blinking against the sudden glare, Paige pulled a wry face as she saw the cord swinging from the centre light. No wonder she hadn't been able to find it!

'Why the interest in the number of blankets?' Kelly's head tilted quizzically to one side. 'You figuring on cutting them up too?'

'No, of course not. I wanted to see if there were enough to make up another bed.'

'You'll be lucky,' he laughed, striding lithely for the door.

'Oh, and what's that supposed to mean?' Her eyes followed him doubtfully even as she began opening the cupboard.

He stopped, sweeping an arm wide, the upward curve to his mouth unbearably provoking. 'See for yourself,' he prompted drily.

Paige scanned the shelves hastily, then checked them a little more slowly to make sure. Oh, no, there was only one! Her thoughts raced onwards. But that might be enough if ...

'You don't happen to have a camp bed or a sleeping bag, do you?' she questioned hopefully.

'Uh-uh!' He shook his head unco-operatively.

'Then would you mind telling me what I'm supposed to do for a bed?' she was forced into demanding sarcastically.

'As there doesn't appear to be much choice in the matter, I guess we do exactly as we're having to do with everything else, Rusty ... we share!'

Green eyes widened incredulously. 'You've got to be joking!' Admittedly the bed was wider than a single, but it certainly wasn't a double!

'Not unless you fancy sleeping on the bare boards.'

'I'd rather do that than share with you!'

'Suit yourself.' He flexed wide shoulders in casual dismissal of the problem and resumed walking.

And so she would, Paige thought furiously. There had to be something suitable she could use to cushion the hardness of the floor. Saddle cloths, towels, the extra sheets—anything would do. But even when she had gathered every last article she could find and had laid them all out neatly she was still ruefully aware that the depth of her improvised mattress wasn't really what one could call inviting. And Kelly's taunting references when he stopped to view her handiwork on his way to the shower definitely hadn't been designed to increase her satisfaction.

'I hope you've thought to keep more than that one blanket for the top,' had been his wry opening comment.

'Why should I?' she had challenged. 'It's not cold.'

'*Now!*' His emphasis had been quite explicit, and then he had gone on to ponder, 'But I wonder if you'll be able to say the same at three o'clock in the morning? It can get very cold during the night out here, even at this time of the year.'

'Well, I—I'll just have to keep warm as best I can, won't I?'

'And *I'll* hope it's successful ... for your sake!' he had smiled goadingly.

A short while later, after turning out the light, Paige slid gingerly between the covers and lay stiffly as she listened to Kelly's carefree whistling penetrating through the wall from the bathroom. When she could stand it no longer—even that sounded mocking to her ears—she rolled on to her side and dragged the blanket higher in an effort to block out the sound. At least in that position the rock-like hardness of her bed wasn't quite so noticeable, she smiled thankfully, and after pushing her pillow into a more comfortable shape —there had been another of those!—she tried every trick she knew to make sleep come more readily.

Unfortunately, none of them were successful, and she was still awake long after Kelly had finished in the bathroom and sought his own bed. She twisted and turned restively, each movement bringing a new protest from muscles which rebelled against such cavalier treatment, and although she slipped into a light doze a few times it was never for long and never restfully. It was even worse, however, when the cold came to plague her as well, for then all her energies were directed towards keeping warm and hopes of any kind of sleep became impossible.

It was while she was pulling the blanket closer to her shivering form that Kelly's muscular shape suddenly loomed up beside her and she realised that dawn wouldn't be long in arriving.

'If you consider you've made your point, would you mind if *I* now get some sleep?' he bit out wrathfully as he disposed of her inadequate covers and, swooping, tossed her effortlessly over a warm bare shoulder. 'Even if you haven't, I've got work to do today and before I tackle it I'd like to have at least *some* time when I'm not having to listen to you moan, groan, squirm, and fidget!'

Paige's objections to his arbitrary action were only halfheartedly voiced. Partly because every forceful

stride he took bounced the breath out of her body, and
partly because after such an uncomfortable and depres-
sing experience she wasn't finding the prospect of sharing a bed quite so intolerable any more.

'I was d-doing all r-right,' she panted.

'Good for you . . . I wasn't!' he snapped as he dumped
her unceremoniously on to the bed and left her to
stare at the broad expanse of his back as he slid in
beside her with economic movements.

Paige put as much distance as possible between them
but still couldn't relax. Her cheek hurt, her shivering
hadn't subsided as yet, and her concealing garment was
bunching annoyingly around her waist.

'For God's sake, what's wrong *now*?' Kelly abruptly
exploded into exasperated life again after her fourth
attempt to straighten her covering.

'I haven't got a pillow, I can't lie on this side because my face hurts too much if I do, and my sheet's
all twisted!' she flared resentfully.

In the deathly silence which followed she could sense
the rigid control he was exercising to restrain his
temper, and then, accompanied by a fervently muttered
epithet, he stormed out of bed and across to the other
room. During his absence she hastily righted her cum-
bersome attire and waited a trifle apprehensively for
his return.

When he did, it was to pace to her side of the bed,
the pillow in his hand being slammed down heavily
behind her, and to issue an order to, 'Move!' in a
tone which brooked no argument.

Paige did so promptly and curled beneath the covers
on the far side of the bed, her limbs beginning to appreciate the warmth seeping back into them at last. A pro-

cess which was greatly increased once the mattress dipped beneath Kelly's weight, for in such a limited area it was impossible for them not to touch, and his body heat quickly erased the remaining chill from her flesh. Certain she wouldn't be able to sleep knowing him to be so disturbingly close, she prepared herself to wait out the rest of the night sleeplessly, but she discovered nature wasn't to be denied so easily and before very long she was drifting into tranquil unconsciousness.

CHAPTER THREE

IT was broad daylight when Paige opened her eyes and came awake hastily, but when a hurried inspection of the room showed her to be completely alone she sighed pleasurably and relaxed back against her pillow, listening. There were no distinguishable sounds coming from the kitchen, or outside, that would indicate Kelly's presence, and tossing off the bedclothes she padded into the spare room to find the watch she had left there the night before. On seeing the time it displayed she grimaced wryly. No wonder he wasn't still around, the morning had half gone already!

Presently, once she was washed and dressed in her own clothes—and feeling a whole lot better because of it—the bed made and her temporary one dismantled, she set about making herself something to wear. Without a pattern cutting out was something of a problem, but as loose-fitting styles were fashionable she didn't think it would matter too much if the finished garments were a little wider than they should have been. It was slow work with no machine available, but towards the end of the afternoon she was feeling quite pleased with what she had been able to accomplish.

Already she had completed a sleeveless blouse with a drawstring neckline, as well as a longer version of the same thing which reached to her knees and which she thought would be suitable to sleep in. One thing was for certain, she wouldn't be wearing that unmanageable sheet to bed again! Also, she had partially finished a wrap-around skirt to team with her blouse and she hoped to have the last stitches in place before the evening was out.

By six o'clock Kelly still hadn't returned and she began taking frequent looks from the verandah to see if he was on his way. Apart from the fact that she knew he had taken Mercury with him—the horse had been missing when she'd retrieved her clothes from the line earlier—she had absolutely no idea in which direction he had gone or for what purpose, and she was becoming rather anxious over the length of time he had been away.

When seven o'clock came round she was already showered and wondering if she shouldn't make some attempt to prepare a meal. However, by now her unease had been replaced by a seething anger. Surely there was no necessity for him to be out so late, and especially when he hadn't even left a note advising his whereabouts. He must know she would be worried! The brute was probably doing it on purpose, she decided fiercely.

After another hour had passed without any sign

of him there was a definite reversal in her attitude, and a mounting fear that something might have happened to him now became her sole consuming thought. It didn't seem to matter now that the dinner she had painstakingly produced was ruining on the stove. Her main worry was that if he didn't return she had no way of advising anyone of the fact. There may have been a transceiver at his disposal, but what was the good of it when she hadn't a clue how to use it? For herself she had no anxieties, the supplies were more than enough to keep her going for a considerable time, and if it became necessary she could wait out the flood until someone was able to rescue her. But Kelly! Even if she could get a message through she wouldn't know where to suggest they look!

Too distracted to concentrate on her sewing, Paige got up to stir the dinner for yet another time and was removing it from the heat altogether when a faint sound attracted her attention. Was that a horse she'd heard? In a flash she was careering across the room and flinging open the door, a heartfelt sigh of relief and thankfulness escaping her to see Kelly dismounting at the yard in the fading light.

Contrarily, though, now that she knew him to be safe her annoyance rapidly returned in full force, and as an ominous buzzing rang in her ears to remind her of the savage mosquitoes, she retreated inside to wait with impatiently drumming fingers for him to enter. When he did so, quite some time later, she wasn't prepared to give him a chance to explain—if, indeed, that had been his intention—but launched right into an attack.

'And where on earth have you been until this hour?'

she demanded heatedly. 'Didn't it occur to you that I might have been frightened to death something had happened to you? You could at least have left a note saying where you'd gone and how long you'd be!'

Kelly took one look at her furious features and burst out laughing. 'My God, she's only been here one day and already she's nagging like a wife! Don't you know you're supposed to wait for at least a few weeks before sounding off like that, Rusty?' he drawled provokingly.

He was acquiring the aggravating knack of using that nickname when she had other, more important, objections to make, she thought vexedly, and this time was no exception.

'Well—I...' It was the gleaming gaze he was directing at her as much as his words which had Paige's colour rising uncontrollably. 'Well, you're not my husband, Kelly Sinclair, so I'll say what I like!' she retorted selfconsciously. 'When you were so late getting home I was sure you'd had an accident and I wouldn't have known where to look for you!'

As he removed his hat and ran a hand roughly through his dark hair he surveyed her measuringly. 'Scared of being left here on your own, were you?' he taunted.

'No! And that...' she blinked rapidly to clear suddenly misty eyes, 'that's a rotten thing to imply. That I was only worried on my own account!'

'In which case, I apologise,' he dipped his head wryly before turning her face up to his with a surprisingly gentle hand. 'But I really didn't intend to be gone so long. Believe it or not, I wasn't altogether unworried about you being here on your own all day either.'

Her eyes registered her amazement. 'But nothing could happen to me here, could it?'

'Something unexpected can always happen,' he declared firmly.

'The more so when I'm around, is that what you're trying to say?'

'Well . . .' The crooked tilt to his mouth set her heart thumping chaotically. 'Your record so far isn't such that it gives a man confidence, Paige Darling.'

She wished he wouldn't say her name like that, it fragmented her thoughts disastrously, and it was some time before she could collect them enough to query, 'Are you ever going to let me live down the fact that I tried to reach Greenvale when I shouldn't have?'

'Perhaps . . . in time,' he teased, his eyes narrowing as they were drawn to the dark discolouration across her cheekbone and a thumb was brushed over the marked skin feather-lightly. 'How is it?'

'Sore and unsightly,' she laughed shakily.

'Never mind, it will only be that shade for a few days.'

'I know, and then it will turn yellow,' she grimaced ruefully.

His consoling smile was accompanied by an arm being draped across her shoulders as he headed towards the stove, sniffing appreciatively. 'Something smells good,' he approved.

Paige shrugged deprecatorily. 'Then I hope it tastes just as nice, because I'm not much of a cook, I'm afraid, and it's been sitting there stewing for quite some time now.'

'After the day I've had, anything would taste okay,' he asserted.

'Oh?' She sent him an enquiring glance as she prepared to ladle out the casserole. She had laid the table hours ago. 'Did you have trouble, after all?'

'Some,' he admitted laconically, making for the hall. 'I'll tell you about it after I've washed.'

He didn't, though, because his dinner was already on the table when he returned and after only one mouthful his thoughts were otherwise occupied.

'Hell!' he shuddered, his expression disbelieving. 'I know we need to keep up our salt intake, but it really isn't necessary for us to have a week's supply all in one meal, you know!'

About to sample it herself for the first time, Paige looked up in dismay. 'Oh, dear, is it too salty? I'm sorry, but I wasn't sure if I put in enough when I started, so I added some more during the cooking.'

'Considerably more, I'd say!'

'I did say I was sorry,' she reminded him defensively. 'And I did warn you that I wasn't much of a hand at cooking. Something like this always seems to go wrong when I get into a kitchen.'

'Then might I suggest we keep you out of the kitchen?' he proposed ironically, rising to his feet and removing their plates. 'How about I do the cooking in future and you do the cleaning up afterwards, eh?'

'But that doesn't seem fair,' she protested. 'I mean, you shouldn't have to work all day and then come in and start preparing meals.'

'That's what I do normally, so what's the difference whether it's for one or two?' he shrugged.

Paige scraped the food thoughtfully off the plates. That was one way of looking at it, she supposed. 'You accept the conditions here very easily, don't you, Kelly?'

she mused. 'Do you prefer it to Ainslie?'

'Sometimes—it all depends.' He carried on with his preparations for their second dinner.

'On whether you have unwanted company or not?'

'You could say that,' he agreed sardonically, and she had to drop her gaze to hide her disappointment.

She had hoped he was beginning to re-assess his estimation of her, but apparently nothing had changed. He had merely been concealing his feelings a little better this evening. In silence she ran hot water into the sink in order to wash up the plates and utensils she had used previously.

'I don't suppose you would know any of the ground-to-air emergency signals, would you, Paige?'

The question came out of the blue and she looked up blankly to query, 'Which signals?'

'Ground-to-air,' he repeated. 'It might have saved you some worry today if you'd known you could signal the emergency service's plane when it flew over this afternoon.'

'Oh, is that whose it was?' she exclaimed comprehendingly. 'I did hear one, but I didn't go outside because I was busy sewing at the time.'

Kelly nodded. 'He would have noted the *"All Well"* signal I laid out last night, anyway, but it might be an idea if I write out a list of some of the more appropriate ones for you, just in case you happen to need them at any time.'

'And just what do you make these signals out of?' she asked.

'Stones, wood, sheets, or anything else you can think of, as long as it's clearly visible from the air,' he advised. 'Marie always made certain Charles had plenty of suitably painted wood available, so you'd have no worries on that score.'

'But how would the pilot know which station was okay and which one wasn't? They must all look alike from up there.' She waved a hand vaguely skywards.

The look he gave her was more than just tinged with mocking disbelief. 'Why else do you think our homesteads have their names emblazoned across their roofs? I can assure you it's not because we have an excess of paint and don't know what else to do with it.'

'Oh, very smart!' she gibed, flushing beneath his satirical regard. 'But as I'm not in the habit of flying over the outback I could hardly be expected to know what you've got on your damned roofs, could I?'

'You've never seen photographs of them taken from the air?' He eyed her quizzically.

'Well, yes, I have,' she admitted grudgingly. Trust him to jog her memory! 'But how was I to know it was a common practice?'

'What *did* you thing it was for, then ... show?'

'I didn't think about it at all, if you must know!' she blazed hotly.

The corners of his mouth pulled in derisively. 'Not thinking is a fundamental characteristic of yours, I gather!'

Paige pressed her lips together furiously, but refused to give him the satisfaction of an attempted denial. 'If you say so,' she managed to shrug, unconcernedly, but still couldn't resist attaching a goading, 'Far be it from me to dispute someone of your apparent omniscience,' as she returned her attention to the dishes in the sink.

'Then it's regrettable you didn't realise that two days ago, isn't it?'

A sparkling glare was sent at the plate Paige was cleaning with unnecessary dedication, but she forbore to retaliate. He had too many weapons at his disposal—not the least of which she had given him herself, she recalled disgustedly—and he obviously wasn't averse to using them. Thus far his feelings towards her only centred around dislike, but it was probably to her own advantage to see they didn't decline any further. She suspected a deliberately alienated Kelly Sinclair would be too corrosive a force to endure, even for the short time she envisaged being at Bindaburra.

Throughout dinner—succulent lamb chops, savoury rice, and tinned vegetables this time—Paige was quiet, her features purposefully composed. Twice tonight he had intimated his dissatisfaction with her presence and she wasn't going to give him a chance to make it three. If he wanted solitude then he could have it, she vowed tartly, oblivious to the fact that her eloquent green eyes were more than effectively doing her talking for her until she moved to make the coffee.

'Are you positive there's nothing else you'd like to add?' Kelly broke the silence in an ironic tone, his eyes following her lazily as she refilled the kettle.

'To what?' Her questioning expression furrowed puzzled creases across her normally smooth forehead.

His attractively shaped mouth twitched wryly. 'The threats and curses you've been raining down on my head all through dinner.'

Good grief, was he a mind-reader too? 'I—I don't know what you're talking about—I haven't said a word,' she protested, albeit a little evasively, and determinedly focussing her eyes elsewhere as she sat the kettle on the stove.

'You didn't have to, those graphic eyes of yours said it all extremely fluently!'

'Oh, that's ridiculous!' she half laughed unsteadily. This was the very thing she had sought to avoid. 'You're letting your imagination run away with you.'

'Am I?' His eyes narrowed watchfully. 'You mean, I haven't been severely castigated and put in my place, been threatened with a cut throat, and then summarily despatched to hell?'

He *was* a mind-reader, she concluded ruefully, and began chewing nervously at her lip.

'Well?' he prompted abruptly.

Unable to gauge the state of his feelings from the timbre of his voice, Paige eventually settled for an innocently tongue-in-cheek, 'Now why would I do something like that?'

'For revenge, most probably.' Kelly's answer came in the form of a laconic drawl as he rose lithely to his feet.

'After all you've done for me?' She succeeded in standing her ground and looking suitably disappointed, even though she would have preferred a swift exit now that he was walking towards her. 'I wouldn't be so ungrateful.'

'Not much you wouldn't!' he countered sarcastically as he came level with her, his hand snaking out to wrap itself amid the long strands of her hair. 'The only reason you're holding back now is because you're not quite certain which way I'll jump if you let fly.'

The fact that he was right in his assumption had Paige throwing caution to the winds and outfacing him rebelliously. 'Oh, I know which way you'd jump all right . . . straight down on me! Why should this time be any different?' she gibed. 'You've done nothing but pick on me ever since we met!'

'Then perhaps you'd better calm that fiery redheaded temper before you provoke me into doing something similar again, hmm?' he proposed softly, but with such a fascinating smile that she could scarcely breathe.

Damn him! She glowered impotently at the broad chest confronting her. If only he hadn't that disturbing ability to set her capricious mind racing off at a tangent whenever she needed all her defences marshalled together! Now, with an irrevocable breach in the protective wall of her anger, she sighed and glanced upwards moodily.

'Why does it always have to be me who backs off? Why not you every once in a while?'

Kelly didn't have to search for a reply, it was ready and waiting, and authoritatively delivered. 'Because you're a headstrong little witch, too used to having your own way, and I reckon it's time someone took you in hand!'

Oh, did he now? Paige's temper started to seethe again and then just as quickly died, replaced by the tempting sensation of challenge.

'I see.' Her eyes gleamed like jewels within their dark silky frames. 'And you've elected yourself to the post of instructor, have you?'

'I guess you could say that,' he concurred drily.

'You're not worried that you might have taken on more than you can handle?' she ventured banteringly. 'That it might turn out to be a case of the master being taught by his pupil?'

A keenly perceptive light entered the depths of the steel-blue eyes holding her gaze so intently, and had Paige swallowing doubtfully when he warned, 'Don't be persuaded into thinking you can twist *me* around your little finger with your feminine wiles, Paige Darling, or you just might find *you're* the one who's taken on more than you can manage.'

A thought which she had studiously tried to ignore until now! 'Mmm, I suppose you're right,' she sighed, and hunched one shoulder in half-hearted resignation. 'It would rather be like attempting the impossible, wouldn't it?'

'Very definitely!' he nodded sharply in emphasis, finally releasing his hold on her and beginning to move away.

Paige stared after him with a considering look on her face. All the same, he could *very definitely* find that taking her in hand wasn't going to be as readily achieved as he thought either!

While they were drinking their coffee Kelly proceeded to make out the list of signals he had previously mentioned, and Paige watched him closely. This was an essential part of living in an isolated area and she was interested to see them for herself.

'Is that all there are?' she asked disappointedly when he had finished writing.

'Not altogether, but I hardly think you'll be wanting to signal such things as *"Require Map and Compass"*, *"Probably Safe to Land"*, or *"Operation Completed"*, etcetera,' he advised ironically. 'These are the only ones you're likely to need.'

Paige scanned the notes swiftly. 'One vertical stroke for *"Require Doctor"*; two vertical strokes for *"Re-*

quire Medical Supplies''; three vertical strokes for *''Require Evacuation''*; a capital **F** for *''Require Food and Water''*; and two capital L's for *''All Well''*,' she mused aloud as she went. At the finish she tipped her head questioning to one side. 'And how big is one supposed to make these figures?'

'Around ten foot or so, certainly no shorter than eight feet in length.'

'Well, that seems straightforward enough,' she nodded. 'But how do I know if the pilot's understood, or even seen the symbols I've laid out?'

'Because he'll indicate that the message has been received and understood by rocking his wings from side to side. Or if the message hasn't been understood he'll make a complete right-hand circuit,' she was informed concisely.

'Mmm, I see.' Thoughtfully she read them through again. 'I still hope I never have to send one. Except for the *''All Well''*, there's a distinctly pessimistic tone to what you've listed here.'

'And all the more so from my standpoint,' Kelly put in ruefully. 'But if it wasn't serious there'd be no necessity for you to be sending any signals at all, because I would be doing it.'

The idea of him being incapacitated to such an extent was not only unpalatable but somehow unnerving as well and, finishing her coffee hastily, Paige took their cups over to the sink in order to start on her second load of washing up.

'Wouldn't it be better if you taught me to use the transceiver instead?' she suggested. 'At least I'd be able to contact Ainslie then if anything unexpected did happen.'

He shook his head negatively, decisively. 'There's no need. Nothing that catastrophic is likely to occur and if you hadn't been stranded here with me I would've managed on my own.'

'It still wouldn't hurt for me to learn, though, would it?' she pressed.

'Maybe not,' he shrugged indifferently, 'but *not* while you're on Bindaburra.'

'But—but why?' Her eyes mirrored her bewilderment. 'I'm not likely to break it, am I?'

'I've already told you why—because there's no need,' he reiterated inflexibly, his mouth a firm level line. 'Besides, we wouldn't want you congesting the air waves every day with long heart-to-heart talks with Stuart!'

Resentment bubbled feverishly inside her. As if she would! She didn't even know him well enough to have heart-to-heart talks with him! Her chin lifted fractionally higher.

'Is that the only reason?' she queried stiffly.

'Isn't it sufficient?' he countered, heavily sarcastic.

'No!' she flared before she could stop herself, but promptly moderated her tone to a less vehement although considerably more subtle inflection. 'I thought it might, perhaps, have been because you didn't want me to talk to anyone at Ainslie.'

'Oh?' Kelly clasped his hands behind his head and leant casually back in his chair. 'And why should it matter to me if you talk to anyone at the homestead or not? You'll be there yourself in a couple of weeks' time and able to talk all you like, so what would be the point?'

Paige shrugged, confounded in the face of such logic,

and turned back to the washing up. That glimmer of suspicion which had temporarily assailed her must have been way off beam, she decided. His remark, however, did prompt other thoughts.

'You said originally that I would be stranded here for five or six weeks,' she recalled tauntingly. 'Has it now been decreased to only two?'

'Only two... at Bindaburra,' he mocked, swinging out of his chair.

'You mean I still won't be able to leave even after we've reached Ainslie?' She watched his approach with dismay.

'Clever girl!' he congratulated sardonically and, tilting her face up to his with a long forefinger beneath her chin, laughed, 'You're really on the ball tonight, aren't you?'

Paige jerked her head backwards before he could guess how calamitously he affected her. 'But I can't stay there all that time uninvited!' she gasped.

'What's the difference whether it's here or there? They're both owned by the same person.'

'It's not the same, though. I don't feel so much like a—a guest here,' she tried to explain selfconsciously.

'Okay, so we'll let you help with the washing up at the homestead too,' Kelly grinned as he picked up the tea towel. 'Will that make you feel any better?'

'It might,' she surprised him by agreeing, and had snatched the towel back out of his hand before he had an opportunity to use it. 'Go and sit down,' she ordered. 'This is my job, you've done yours.' Then, with an enquiring look, '*Would* it be possible for me to repay some of what I'll owe your boss for my keep, etcetera, by working while I'm there?'

Kelly hooked his fingers into the back of his wide belt and seated himself on the corner of the table, one long leg swinging free. 'Well, there are two vacancies at the moment,' he divulged thoughtfully. 'Although I don't really think either of them would be entirely suitable for you.'

'Why not?'

A chaffing curve swept the corners of his attractive mouth upwards. 'Because one's for a married stockman, and the other's for a mechanic.'

Distracted for a moment, Paige forgot her annoyance caused by his deliberate misleading as she repeated, 'A mechanic! Whatever do they want one of those for out here?'

'Oh, nothing important,' he discounted drily. 'Just to maintain the station's vehicles, graders, windmills, engines, pump heads, borehole pumps, and any other assorted machinery I might have missed, that's all.'

'Well, how was I supposed to know that?' She turned her back on him huffily. 'You shouldn't have been so ready to make fun of me when I was only looking for some method to help pay my way. I don't want to be indebted to your boss all that time.'

'Of course it would be different if you were on Greenvale, wouldn't it?' he drawled meaningfully behind her.

'Yes, it would!' Her answer was unconditional. 'I received an invitation to visit that property. I wouldn't have been just landing myself on them like I have done here!' And almost sensing what he was about to say next, she whirled around, unmindful of the water dripping from her hands on to the floor, to forestall him by threatening, 'And don't you dare say, "Then you should have thought of that before ignoring my advice"!'

'It would never have occurred to me,' he disclaimed with a laugh—a deep-toned, captivating sound which had Paige staring at him defencelessly as her insides began looping the loop with gay abandon. It wasn't fair, she railed mutely. No man should have as much going for him as this one did. 'But if it's only an invitation you're waiting for,' it took her a while to realise he was continuing, 'then allow me to hereby issue you with one,' he offered, bending gallantly low.

'Thank you,' she half smiled wistfully. It was the first time he had attempted to make her feel better, not worse, over her self-inflicted troubles. 'But it's not really up to you to issue one, is it? Your boss is the only one who can do that.'

The grey of his eyes was strikingly conspicuous for a scant second and then it disappeared. 'Don't be an idiot!' he reproved roughly. 'Everyone knows you're here and they'll be expecting me to take you across to Ainslie as soon as it's possible. At a time like this it's just accepted that you'll stay in the homestead.'

'I see.' Reconciled, although still not altogether content, she picked up the tea towel and began drying one of the plates, her head downbent as she asked hesitantly, 'Will you be staying at the station once we get there, or—or will you be coming straight back here?'

'That depends on too many things for me to give a reply right now.' He lowered his head slightly to obtain a clearer view of her pensive face. 'Why, were you hoping to have one familiar face around ... or vice versa?'

'The latter, naturally!' she retaliated in the same

bantering tone, her eyes holding his bravely.

'That's what I thought.' His endorsement was wryly made.

Before she gave him reason to revise his opinion, Paige hastily sought to turn his thoughts in another direction. 'If, in a couple of weeks, we can make it from here to Ainslie without any trouble, why can't I make it back to Sydney as well?' she puzzled.

'Mainly because of the lie of the land,' he smiled. 'Although it's not particularly noticeable to the naked eye, there is a definite gradient which makes it possible for us to reach the head station once the water level has fallen to some degree, but from there to the highway the opposite occurs and, consequently, that area is one of the last to be cleared of water.'

'Couldn't I make it back to Tingala from here by the same route I used to arrive?'

Kelly shook his head slowly, but purposefully. 'You're forgetting the creek, aren't you? It will be quite some time before a vehicle can cross that safely again.'

This time Paige accepted the seemingly inevitable, but mention of that now turbulent waterway immediately reminded her of another problem and she voiced it anxiously.

'What will happen about my car, Kelly?'

'By that I take it you mean, are you likely to get it back again?' he quizzed.

She nodded, her heart skipping a beat. She hadn't realised there might be a possibility of her not getting it back at all!

'Then I'm afraid the answer is no,' he replied quietly, his expression unusually gentle. 'Rather than attempt to recover it, have it stripped down and completely rebuilt, you're better off abandoning it altogether and buying another one.'

Her shoulders slumped dejectedly as she assimilated this devastating piece of information and it became necessary for her to swallow hard before she was able to enquire huskily, 'And m-my luggage?'

Kelly raked a hand savagely through his dark hair. 'If it hasn't been washed away, I doubt most of it will be worth having,' he informed her brusquely.

Paige could only nod her acknowledgment, unable to meet the penetrating gaze she was all too aware hadn't moved from her, and rapidly put down the plate she had been holding in order to pick up another and rub the towel over it jerkily. No car, no clothes, no money! The words kept pounding through her head in a distressing refrain.

Suddenly both the towel and the plate were removed from her hands and she found herself held reassuringly against a hard chest and a soothing hand cradling her head.

'It was a costly lesson for you to learn, wasn't it, Rusty?' he murmured.

Long wet lashes encircled eyes of a deep shimmering green. 'The most expensive Picnic Races and Grand Ball I've ever proposed attending,' she half laughed, half cried.

'Oh, hell!' His arms tightened instinctively. 'Why didn't you stay in town where you belong!'

It wasn't a question so much as a rejection of her presence and she had to bite hard at her lip to stop its trembling betrayal of her hurt. 'You m-might at least pretend to t-tolerate me considering what I p-paid for the honour of being here,' she charged plaintively on a sob of desolation.

'Like this?' he queried deeply as his firmly-moulded mouth closed over hers.

Yes! cried her unruly senses, responding openly to the sensuous caress. No! shouted her brain, attempting to deny his attraction.

Caught somewhere between the two, Paige could only whisper an indecisive 'N-no,' and pray Kelly wasn't aware of the confusion his exploring lips were creating.

Seconds later she was put firmly away from him. 'I think perhaps I'd better head for the shower before tolerance is supplanted by indulgence,' he smiled crookedly. 'Thrust together as we are, things could easily get out of control without our intending, or even realising, it was happening.'

'Yes, I suppose so,' she agreed awkwardly, keeping her eyes fixed to the floor and only raising them once he had left.

It had been a disturbing experience in more ways than one and she didn't think it would be prudent to repeat it either! Kelly Sinclair already had too strong an impact on her emotions without her inadvisedly giving him the chance to increase it.

When he returned she had finished the drying up and was absorbed with her sewing again, and although she would have preferred him to break the somewhat taut silence which existed, there was something she wanted to know and she tried to speak as naturally as possible.

'Have you—er—contacted the homestead yet to-night?' she asked, speculating that he might have done so after his shower.

'No, I was in touch with them this morning instead,' he revealed levelly. 'I won't be calling them again now until tomorrow.'

That he could appear so unaffected by what had happened gave Paige the encouragement to continue. 'Did you remember to pass on that message for me?'

'That's why I called in early. I thought you would rather your parents received news of you as soon as possible.'

'Yes, I would, thank you,' she smiled shyly. At least that was one of her worries taken care of. 'How long do you think it will be before it reaches them?'

'They should have it by now, I sent it as a telegram,' he relayed absently as he poured himself a cup of coffee from the pot simmering on the stove. Then, still holding it aloft, he arched his brows meaningfully in her direction.

'Yes, please,' she laughingly accepted his unspoken offer, and when he repeated the gesture with a packet of cigarettes he took from his shirt pocket she nodded emphatically, *'Yes, please!'*

The little byplay served to clear the air and the cigarette eased her nervousness so that she was able to sit across the table from him with her previous tension fast disappearing.

'You've managed to make yourself something, I see.' Kelly indicated her sewing.

'Mmm, they're not exactly what one would call high fashion, but they're better than nothing,' she smiled.

After watching her industriously ply her needle for a few moments his curiosity seemed to get the better of him. 'Just what is it?' he probed drily.

'It's a skirt ... see?' she chuckled as she rose to her feet and quickly wrapped it around herself in a demonstration.

'Isn't it supposed to have a belt of some kind?' he was swift to realise after an astute survey.

'Yes, well, they do normally have ties,' she admitted. 'But I thought I might cheat and see if you have a large safety pin I could use instead to save me the bother of making them.'

'There should be one in the medicine kit you can have,' he disclosed offhandedly. 'Is that all you've made so far?'

Paige shook her head vigorously. 'No, I've also made a blouse to go with this skirt, and something a little more comfortable to sleep in,' she imparted her information with no little satisfaction.

'Good, I'm glad to hear it!' His words were no less pleased. 'It felt as if I was sleeping next to a mummy last night.'

'At least you can be grateful you weren't the one having to wear it!' she rushed into retorting as a rosy pink flush climbed into her cheeks.

'It seemed as if I was when I woke up this morning,' he returned sardonically. 'For a time I thought I was being attacked by a cocoon.'

Uncertain whether to laugh or to defend herself, she finally chose the latter. 'Oh, it couldn't have been that bad! It might have become a little untidy, but I certainly still had it wrapped around me when *I* woke up!'

'With my compliments only!' His accompanying bow was mockingly executed.

Paige stared at him in growing embarrassment. 'You mean, it had become partially unravelled during the night?' she queried tentatively.

'Wholly, would be a more accurate description, I believe.'

The pink flush became a crimson tide. 'I wasn't wearing it at all when you woke up?' she despairingly enquired the worst.

Even if his slowly shaking head hadn't told her the answer the provoking curve to his mouth would have. 'Not a stitch,' he drawled lazily.

'So you p-put it back around m-me?' she stammered. Her skin couldn't colour any darker, but she could certainly feel it getting hotter.

'I thought you would prefer it,' he owned drily.

Paige's thoughts weren't nearly so confident! Her only consolation was the fact that she hadn't been awake to witness the mortifying discovery, and that it wasn't likely to happen again now that she had something more fitting to wear. Without that knowledge she doubted whether she would have had the nerve to go near the bed again!

CHAPTER FOUR

ONE morning towards the end of her first week Paige awoke much earlier than usual and didn't bother trying to go back to sleep again but lay there musing complacently. Five days ago she wouldn't have believed it possible that she could wake like this to find a man's arm resting heavily across her body, the fingers spread wide over her midriff, and be so utterly unperturbed by the discovery.

The first time she had regained consciousness during the night and found herself held prisoner so securely had disturbed her considerably, she had to admit, but when no further movement had eventuated she had gradually relaxed again and gone back to sleep. She didn't know whether the action was just the automatic result from the way Kelly slept—most times on his stomach with one arm thrown out wide—or whether it was a carryover from the days when he had been married. Whatever the cause it was a recurring habit now, she smiled, and one she found strangely comforting.

Slipping carefully on to her back so as not to trouble the man beside her, she turned her head slightly so that she could study him more closely. He slept easily, totally relaxed, his dark hair tousled forward over his wide forehead, his well-cut mouth curving engagingly. Slowly her eyes travelled past the powerful shoulders to the muscled width of his back, the tan of his skin showing abnormally dark against the sheets in the half light. She guessed the shorts he wore to bed were in consideration of herself, since she had seen no sign of any pyjamas during her stay, and had long since concluded that he usually preferred to sleep without them.

Her thoughts wandered on unhindered. The better she came to know him, the more she failed to understand why his wife would have wanted a divorce. True, he could be infuriating at times, and there was a hint of ruthlessness there which presaged disaster for anyone imprudent enough to underrate him, but she would still have to rate him as one of the most interesting and appealing males she had ever met.

Too appealing on occasion, she recollected wryly.

Although he had made no move, or shown signs of wanting to repeat that one brief kiss he had given her, she had often found herself traitorously half wishing that he would. Ever since their first meeting he'd had an unsettling influence on her emotions which, unfortunately for her, she grimaced, wasn't lessening as the days passed.

She twisted restively as if to physically dispel her disconcerting contemplations, but when the hand resting across her waist took exception to the movement by tightening its grasp, she desisted and lay still again. What had his wife been like? Her mind returned to its original subject as if drawn by a magnet. Had she been bred in the outback or had she come from town and discovered the life to be too lonely and restricting for her? Was that why they had divorced? Because, like the wife of the previous owner of Bindaburra, she hadn't been able to stand the isolation?

In Paige's case, much to her surprise, she was finding the emptiness wasn't bothering her as much as she had expected it to, and each day she felt herself becoming more firmly attracted to the immensity of the remorseless terrain which surrounded them. She was willing to allow that perhaps Kelly's presence had more than a little to do with her untroubled state, though. With someone so forceful and seemingly indestructible around it could have been difficult not to feel safe and invulnerable... except from the man himself, of course, she couldn't resist adding with a grin.

'You're awake early this morning.' Kelly's voice suddenly sounded lazily beside her. 'And very pleased about it too, if your expression's anything to judge by.'

The grin widened into a delightful smile. 'I was just thinking about the outback.'

'And smiling?' His voice registered disbelief.

'Why not?' she asked in all seriousness, turning to look at him. 'I like what I've seen of it so far.'

'Even though it's already robbed you of all your possessions and is likely to continue keeping you a reluctant captive for untold weeks?'

'Yes, even so,' she nodded definitely. 'Why shouldn't I?'

'No reason, except that it's an unusual attitude for a city slicker to take, and especially a female one,' he drawled.

'Well, maybe my roots aren't so irrevocably entrenched in the city as you apparently like to think,' she mocked. And because the opportunity had presented itself, 'Is that why you and your wife split up?'

'Because your roots aren't entrenched in the city?' One eyebrow flicked upwards whimsically.

'No!' She sent him a speaking glance. 'I meant because she didn't like the outback, of course!'

Kelly rolled over on to his back, his expression edged with irony as he clasped his hands beneath his head and stared up at the ceiling.

'I don't think Nadine even realised most of the time that she *was* living in the outback,' he revealed wryly.

'Oh?' Paige's brows were the ones to wing higher now. Well, that settled that question, she grimaced inwardly. But what to ask next? His reply had truly left her with nothing to say. Luckily, he continued of his own accord, however, and she listened closely.

'The only thing that worried Nadine was whether she could impress all her friends by entertaining on a sufficiently grand scale or not,' he went on in the same dry tone. 'She wasn't satisfied with luncheons and dinner parties and the occasional guest. She had a hankering for morning coffees, afternoon teas, and champagne breakfasts as well—together with the resident guests to attend them all, of course!'

Champagne breakfast! Good lord, whatever had the woman been thinking of? 'And you couldn't afford all that, naturally enough?' she surmised aloud.

His eyes flickered briefly and then he corrected, 'I couldn't *stand* all that! It became impossible to move in the house without stumbling over one of Nadine's so-called guests. *Guests!*' he repeated with a disparaging sound at the back of his throat. 'Half of them were nothing but damned freeloaders looking for someone to support them!'

'So you finally exploded and threw them all out,' Paige stated the obvious. She just couldn't imagine him doing anything else.

'And her along with them!'

'You didn't!' she gasped. Now *that* she hadn't anticipated.

'Oh, yes, I did!' she was informed without the slightest sign of regret. 'I figured five years of it was enough for anyone to have to take.'

'But you still can't throw out a wife as if she was a— a piece of unwanted junk!' she expostulated.

'Don't worry, I told you she was as happy to go as I was to see her leave,' he laughed at her horrified face. 'If she couldn't have her sycophants around her then she wasn't interested in staying.'

Of all the shallow, empty-headed . . . ! How could anyone be so blind as to throw away gold in order to chase after gilt? Paige denounced incredulously. A moment later, having retraced their conversation and coupled it with a previous remark, she fixed him with an anxious frown.

'Did you *used* to own a property before you were married, Kelly?' she asked softly.

Even white teeth gleamed in a slow, lazy smile. 'If you're thinking I let my wife send me bankrupt then you don't know me very well, Paige Darling,' he taunted.

'I—I just thought it could have happened, after what you said,' she murmured, hunching away self-consciously from his gaze.

'Well, it didn't, because the answer to your question is, no, I did not own a property before I was married,' he relayed openly.

As he was in such an expansive and agreeable mood Paige decided to push her luck a little further by asking, 'Your wife wasn't a native of the outback then?'

He shook his head. 'No, she came from the city, like you.'

'And is that where you met her, in the city?'

'No, it was at Ainslie.'

Not nearly so affable now, she noted, but still chanced, 'She was one of Mr Morgan's guests, was she?'

'Not that I recall.'

'Then how...'

'Then how about we drop the subject, hmm?' he cut in sardonically, his co-operativeness coming to a decided halt. 'After all, I don't continually probe into your personal life, do I?'

'Why should you?' she countered airily in an effort to alleviate her sinking feeling of deflation. He obviously wasn't even interested enough to ask! 'There's nothing particularly spellbinding about a suburban secretary.'

'But there is about my marriage?'

'I was only being polite and displaying a casual in-

terest,' she prevaricated, discomfited, as she tossed back
the covers and flounced out of bed. 'How was I to know
I was treading on sacred ground?'

'By keeping your pretty little nose out of my business!'

The deliberate snub bit deep and, as a result, Paige's
chin angled belligerently. 'Well, I didn't ask for all that
information, don't forget! You volunteered most of
it!'

'Only to save you the trouble.'

'You're too kind!' she gibed acidly, the perspicacity
and the amusement in his voice grating unbearably.
'But just so you're not tempted to be quite so mag-
nanimous another time, that sort of rebounding
favour I can well do without, thanks all the same!'

His indolent shrug in response did nothing to soothe
her ruffled feelings, however, and with one last haughty
sniff she whirled and headed for the bathroom. This
was apparently going to be one of his infuriating days,
she muttered caustically to herself. It was always the
same. He would allow her just so much latitude with
her questioning and then, bang! he erected a wall that
was impossible to break through. Why? That was something she hadn't been able to fathom as yet, because it
wasn't only queries of a personal nature that he took
exception to at times, it was those relating to his work
as well. To date she'd had no recourse but to suppose
it was due to his normally being a very private type
of person. What other solution could there be?

By mid-morning Paige had finished her usual tidying
up and sweeping inside the house and was ready to set
off on her daily inspection of the perimeter of their

dry knoll. Up until yesterday the water level had been gradually mounting towards its peak and she was eager to see whether it was still at the same height today or whether it had dropped slightly, as Kelly had predicted it would.

The sun was turning the surrounding water into a brilliantly reflecting mirror which threw back the light in a myriad colours as she stepped from the porch to the beaten earth below and she had, of necessity, to keep her eyes focussed on the ground a few feet in front of her in order to avoid the unrelenting glitter. Past untended gardens and a huge shading bauhinia she soon left the small building behind and began walking through the thick stand of trees and scrub which had been her first sight of Bindaburra.

Here it was pleasantly shaded and she was glad of the opportunity to lift her head and gaze about her. Especially so when a few minutes later a crashing through the undergrowth eventuated into a huge bull suddenly appearing ahead of her on the track. During the days they had been marooned at the outstation a number of animals had arrived at varying intervals to join them in their solitude, and Paige had soon discovered they were even more wary of her than she was of them.

However, there was something different about this one, she decided on second inspection, once she had recovered from her first startled step backwards. Not only was his hide not smooth and sleek like the others— his was matted and scarred—but he also possessed a mean pair of bloodshot eyes which were regarding her unwaveringly and the most evil set of viciously curving horns she had ever seen. When the great head lowered and he started to paw at the ground with his right hoof she knew immediately that her sixth sense hadn't let her down with its warning that all was not well, and she did two things simultaneously. She looked about her frantically for something that might offer shelter and she screamed as loudly as she could for Kelly. He was working around the homestead somewhere, she knew, but whether he was within calling range or not was another matter.

In the next instant both of them moved in unison, the bull heading unerringly for Paige, while she took off at a tangent for the nearest tree with a conveniently located fork in its trunk. Fear must have leant wings to her feet, for she never knew how she made it over all the obstacles in time, but with a thankful prayer that she was wearing her slacks and not a hampering skirt, she leapt for the tree and scrambled feverishly upwards out of harm's way even as the bull ploughed into the trunk below her. Almost shaken from her precarious position, and fearing another onslaught, she wrapped her arms tightly around the closest branch and screamed again for Kelly. Her fervent hope was that the sound would carry in the still, silent atmosphere.

Snorting and pawing at the base of the tree, the hulking beast was obviously working itself up into a fine rage and the second attack on her defenceless and not overly sturdy haven produced an ominous crack which had Paige turning deathly white and opening her mouth to call for help a third time. A cry which had no need to be uttered, she realised with a heartfelt 'Thank God!' on seeing Kelly galloping towards them astride a barebacked Mercury with a rifle held in one hand.

'You do get yourself into some unhealthy predica-
ments, don't you, Paige Darling?' he drawled wryly,
sizing up the situation.

'I'm glad you find it amusing!' she blazed back across
the intervening space, her gratitude rapidly succumbing to resentment. 'But instead of making fun of me,
why don't you...' With a gasp she broke off to shout
his name in panic-stricken warning as the bull turned
its attention to a more accessible foe.

The immobile calmness with which both man and
horse faced the charging animal had Paige catching her
breath and clapping a hand fearfully to her mouth,
expecting the worst, but it could only have been seconds
before Kelly had aimed and fired at the thundering
beast, dropping him in his tracks like a proverbially
pole-axed steer.

It all happened so quickly that for a moment she
found it hard to believe the menacing form had been
so speedily reduced to a twitching carcass, and as Kelly
urged his mount towards her tree she called out
anxiously,

'Are you sure he's dead?'

'As dead as he's ever likely to be. Come and take a
look for yourself,' he invited with a smile.

Still not moving from her perch and continuing to
eye the lifeless body nervously, she shook her head
quickly. 'What made him act like that? Was he sick?'
she worried over the animal's behaviour.

'No, he's just a scrubber—one of the herd that's
managed to evade being mustered for a few years and
reverted to the wild. They can grow pretty cagey once
they've managed to give the stockman the dodge the
first time.'

'Are there many like that?'

'I hope not.' His glance was extremely dry. 'The men are paid to muster them, not to miss them.'

'Oh, I see,' she murmured embarrassedly. She hadn't intended to cast aspersions on anyone's efficiency. 'What will you do with him now, just leave him there?'

'Seeing this is the direction most of our breezes come from I don't really think you'd appreciate it if I did,' he grinned. 'No, as it's easy towing from here I'll hitch him up to the Land Cruiser and drag him over the other side of the hill where he'll be out of sight and, more importantly, out of smelling reach as well.' As he came to a halt beside her tree his eyes, a vivid blue at the moment, flicked over her humorously. 'It seems it's becoming a habit for you to need rescuing from high perches.'

'Well, it was a damned sight better than being trampled underfoot by that brute!' she defended herself heatedly, all the while trying to combat the wayward pull of her emotions at the magnetic picture Kelly made as he sat Mercury with such ease, one hand spread across a slim hip, the other still grasping the rifle upright and the butt resting on a powerfully muscled thigh.

'You could be right,' he teased. 'At least you didn't try to outrun him, or to hide behind the biggest tree you could find.'

Paige's widening eyes showed her surprise. 'As a matter of fact, I did consider hiding behind that one over there,' she admitted, pointing out a multi-stemmed native orange.

'Then it's just as well you changed your mind, or

else we might not have been able to have this conversation.'

'I thought that would be the next best thing!' she exclaimed, aghast as the import of his words came home to her.

Kelly moved his head in flat denial. 'Surprising as it may seem, you would have found that he could get around a large trunk like that much faster than you could. So, if you have no option but to seek such protection, then make sure you choose a more slender tree —one that gives *you* the advantage, not him.'

'Wouldn't they just try to bulldoze it out of the way like he did?'

'Not usually, not while he can see you're still on the ground.'

'You keep saying "he" all the time,' she noticed with a frown. 'Don't cows ever go wild like that too?'

'Occasionally,' he agreed with wry overtones. 'But like most females they're usually more biddable and less aggressive than the male.'

'I see.' Her green eyes flashed impudently and she just had to goad, 'So you do admit to having some faults, then?'

The slanting look she received in return had her heart pounding raggedly. 'You keep that up and before very long you're likely to discover just how many,' he threatened in a lazy drawl. 'Now, do you want a ride back to the house or not?'

'On him?' She eyed Mercury dubiously. 'No, thanks, I've only just recovered from my last effort. Besides, I was intending to take my daily constitutional around our island to see if the water level's begun to fall yet.'

'Can't wait to reach more congenial company and surroundings, eh?'

There, he'd done it again! That totally unpredictable switch from banter to derision which was becoming almost as regular as his about-faces regarding her questions. And, as always, her only defence was to agree mockingly, which she did with a flippant nonchalance.

'Why not? It is what I came for, after all.'

'Then you'll be pleased to learn that it's dropped by a couple of inches since yesterday,' he advised sardonically.

'Oh, good,' Paige played her part to the full. 'At this rate it shouldn't be too long before we can make it to Ainslie.'

'Except that I wouldn't rush my fences if I were you,' he taunted. 'If we leave too soon it will become a case of our having to dig the vehicle out every mile or so. Even four-wheel-drives become bogged if the conditions are bad enough, you know.'

She shrugged disinterestedly. 'Oh, well, I'm sure I can safely leave that decision to you, knowing you won't keep us here any longer than is absolutely necessary.'

'What brought you to that conclusion?'

'Why, the indisputable fact that you dislike me being here only a little less than you dislike me personally, of course!'

'Oh, I don't know.' He ran his eyes over her appraisingly. 'The bed isn't nearly so warm at night when you're not around.'

Paige pursed her lips angrily. Not only was this his second reversal in as many minutes but he'd managed to make her blush with embarrassment into the bar-

The Mills & Boon 🌹 Romance Club

The Romance Club brings love and intrigue, jealousy and passion into your home. Every month you'll receive — post free — the latest romances by the world's best loved romantic novelists, which *only* Mills & Boon can bring you.

Join many other lovers of Mills & Boon Romances who already enjoy the benefits of being a member of the Romance Club. As a member you will enjoy:

★ Your own free monthly club newsletter packed with information about the latest Mills & Boon titles and your favourite authors.

★ Exclusive special money-saving offers.

★ Free express delivery of your new books straight to your home.

Take advantage of our special introductory offer and receive your first 10 books for only £1!

After that you need only take one more selection of books for *just* £6.50 post free. Then, for as long as you wish to remain a member, we shall send you an exciting parcel of 10 new Mills & Boon Romances every month, for only £6.50 all post free.

But if at any time during your membership you decide not to keep your most recent selection of books, simply return them to us in perfect condition and your membership will be cancelled immediately.

To get your 10 new Mills & Boon Romances — for only £1 — just complete the pre-paid reply card and post it to us today!

- -

Postage will
be paid by
Mills & Boon
Limited

Do not affix postage stamps if posted in Gt. Britain, Channel Islands or N. Ireland.

|2|

BUSINESS REPLY SERVICE
Licence No. CN.81

MILLS & BOON READER SERVICE, P.O. Box 236, Thornton Road, Croydon, Surrey CR9 9EL.

gain! Striving to appear unaffected by this new aggravation, she allowed herself a wry grimace and refused to drop her gaze.

'Well, isn't that nice?' she gibed sarcastically. 'Words couldn't possibly convey how honoured it makes me feel just knowing my presence hasn't been totally unacceptable, and that in my own small inadequate fashion I did somehow manage to bring a little comfort into your life!'

'Along with the exasperation, vexation, and provocation, you mean?' One eyebrow crooked quizzically above a mocking blue glint.

'Naturally!' She opened her eyes facetiously wide. 'Not even you can expect to have everything your own way. You must be prepared to take the bad with the good the same as everyone else has to.'

'Thanks for reminding me, although I don't really think I was in any danger of forgetting,' he drawled.

'Not while I'm here, anyway!'

He didn't bother answering but simply inclined his head acknowledgingly—which to Paige's mind was a more pointed corroboration than any words could have been—and then chafed, 'Seeing you appear loath to leave that tree and have no further need of my assistance, I'll be getting back to my work.'

As her reluctance to return to the ground had been prompted by an unwillingness to place herself at a disadvantage by having to look so far up to him, Paige saw no reason to alter her thinking at this stage and still made no effort to move. His remark did, however, occasion a pang of guilt and she set about erasing it a trifle uncomfortably.

'Yes, well, I apologise for not thanking you earlier

for coming to my rescue. I think he must have taken instant exception to my red hair, because he certainly seemed most determined to dispose of me,' she half laughed, and shuddered at the same time.

Kelly heeled Mercury closer and reached out towards her with a muscular brown arm. 'Come on, you can give your constitutional a miss for today,' he said, his tone strangely rough to her ears.

Grudgingly, she allowed herself to be helped down to the fork and from there she eyed him doubtfully. 'But I enjoy my walks,' she protested, although not very forcefully. 'And—and they're interesting.'

'Today's included?'

'Well, it was certainly different,' she smiled faintly.

'Too different for you, I'm thinking, Rusty.' The shapely mouth crooked lazily. 'You look somewhat on the shaken side to me.'

'Would you wonder!' she demanded expressively. 'The experience was a trifle on the nerve-racking side, to say the least!'

'Which is exactly why I'm suggesting you leave it for today. Even if you're not nervous about what you might happen to stumble on to next ... *I am!*'

'Because it would ruin your reputation if anything happened to me since everyone knows I'm here and supposedly in your care?' she proposed ironically.

Before she knew what was happening his helping hand had suddenly become a constricting hand as it slid around her waist and she was whisked off her feet and on to Mercury's back with perfect ease.

'Because I wouldn't want anything to deprive me of the satisfaction of making certain you collect your just dues one of these days, Paige Darling,' he lowered his head to amend softly.

'In other words, if there's any trampling to be done, you prefer to do it yourself!' she retorted throatily, his sentiments far less disturbing than his nearness, Why was it that when he was asleep and had his arm thrown around her—much the same as now—she found it comforting, and yet when he was awake it was an infinitely disconcerting contact?

'Especially when it's innocent-looking redheads who like to trade on their big, beautiful green eyes to charm people out of their convictions,' he confirmed in the same lazy tone.

'Then I have nothing at all to worry about, have I?' she mocked in an attempt to convince herself. 'Whoever heard of anyone being able to charm open the jaws of a steel trap? I wouldn't even be misguided enough to try!'

'No?'

'*No!*' she denied vehemently. 'Why should it matter to me what you think?'

'What else would prompt all those looks of pseudo-hurt innocence whenever I mention Stuart?'

'Maybe because they weren't feigned at all!' she rounded on him caustically. 'Or didn't that ever occur to you?'

'No, I can't say it did,' he returned blandly.

Paige sighed defeatedly. 'I think I will go for my walk after all, thanks,' she murmured, and made as if to slip to the ground, but his securing arm forestalled the movement and she was caught back against him even more tightly.

'That idea's already been vetoed for today, remember?'

'Well, I'm not staying here so he,' she nodded towards Mercury's proud head as he obediently continued on his way, 'can punish one end while you verbally attack the other!' she gritted, trying to prise herself free. And when all her efforts proved futile, 'Let go of me, Kelly! You've got no right to keep me up here.'

'Some say, "Might is right",' he laughed goadingly.

'But I don't happen to be one of them!' she flared, and jabbed an elbow backwards into his ribs in a more forceful bid for freedom.

There was an indistinct exclamation and then it was the hand holding the rifle which was keeping her in place while Kelly's other grasped Mercury's mane and he urged the horse into a bone-shaking gallop—for Paige, anyway—over the remaining yards to the house. No sooner had they come to a halt than he had dismounted, rested the firearm against the fence post, and stood with his hands on his hips looking up at her with a challenging expression.

'Now let's see how brave you are while we've both got our hands free, shall we?' he taunted.

As uneasy as she was, Paige was determined she wasn't going to apologise. Why should she? If he'd let her go for her walk as she had first suggested it wouldn't have been necessary for her to have hit out as she did. She shifted nervously but made no move to dismount.

'It was your own fault,' she blustered. 'And—and besides . . .' she cast about desperately for something to distract him, 'I thought you were supposed to be taking care of me.'

'Don't worry, I'm about to,' promised Kelly as a hand snaked out to catch at her forearm.

Feeling herself losing her balance, Paige clutched a handful of mane which had the effect of making Mercury swing his hindquarters towards Kelly, but as the inexorable pressure on her arm finally had her releasing her grip and sliding downwards the horse collided with both of them, knocking them sideways so that Kelly hit the ground on his back with Paige sprawled over the top of him.

'Are—are you all right?' she immediately enquired on an anxious note. He had cushioned her fall but that had, perforce, made his landing doubly hard.

A provoking light shone in the depths of his blue-grey eyes and a heart-stirring smile traced its way across firmly shaped lips. 'It's not quite what I had in mind, but I'm not complaining,' he drawled as strong arms stole smoothly around her, preventing any moves to rise.

All too embarrassingly conscious of her position, and the lean rugged frame beneath her, Paige spared him one deeply resentful, deeply green glare and renewed her efforts. But when a warm hand slid under her long hair to cup the back of her head, an unavoidable pressure forcing it downwards, there was no time to offer more than a strangled, 'No!' of panicking dissent before her lips were relentlessly claimed.

Now she knew why she had only been *half* wishing Kelly would kiss again! He attracted, yet made her apprehensive at the same time, and it was far too simple a matter for him to arouse emotions she would rather keep dormant for her to wholeheartedly want him to repeat the experience too often.

His mouth was searing hers with a compelling dominance—hard and determined, brooking no evasion—and as much as she tried to fight against it the outcome was inevitable. On a tremulous sigh of surrender, her breath mingled with his, her lips parted of their own accord and she found herself answering the persuasive demand of his mouth with a fervour matched only by the fiery blaze of desire rioting through her bloodstream.

Without releasing either her lips or his grasp, Kelly swung her on to her back, bearing his weight on one elbow as he leant over her, his mouth marking a burning trail as it roamed over the receptive skin of her cheeks and throat before returning to her waiting lips again.

Then suddenly, with a muffled sound of disbelief and a quick shake of his head—which Paige couldn't decide whether had been directed at her uninhibited response or his own impulsive action—he laid a last absorbing kiss to the corner of her mouth and levered himself into a sitting position.

'I'm sorry, I shouldn't have taken advantage of our situation like that,' he apologised ruefully. 'As I said, it wasn't what I originally intended.'

Paige scurried to her feet and shrugged with forced indifference as she began combing unsteady fingers through her hair. 'It doesn't matter, I guess we're probably just suffering from the same complaint. Propinquity's what they call it, isn't it?'

'Mmm,' came the laconic concurrence as he rose agilely upright beside her. 'That's one way of describing it.'

'Is there any other?' She slanted him a wide-eyed look of naïvety.

'Oh, yes, there are others,' he stated definitely, his return glance wryly assessing.

'But none that apply in our case,' she hastened to assert. That gaze had been too shrewdly knowledgeable for her peace of mind. 'I mean, we don't even like each other very much, do we?'

'Perhaps it's just as well.' His mouth took on a humorous twist. 'If we had, who knows how we may have chosen to demonstrate our feelings.'

'Exactly the point I'm making,' she argued, and flushed as she avoided looking at him. 'Our actions were only dictated through our living in such close proximity, not by—by . . .'

'Desire?'

'*Partiality* was the word I was thinking of, actually!'

'No matter,' he grinned, and patted her cheek annoyingly. 'The intent's much the same even if the spelling's different.'

Paige pressed her lips together in vexation but let the purposely antagonistic remark ride. So far she was just managing to hold her ground, but she couldn't guarantee she would be capable of continuing that way if she was tempted to answer in kind, as he was no doubt anticipating her doing.

Instead she changed the subject entirely and had the pleasure of taking him completely by surprise as she asked, 'How long will it take us to reach the homestead when we do leave?'

'A day if we're lucky, two if we're not,' he shrugged, recovering quickly. 'It depends on how wet the ground still is and how many detours we have to make.'

'So it's quite a way?'

'Not really, just over sixty miles.'

'And will we be travelling on Bindaburra for most of the time?' Her brows peaked enquiringly.

'Only for the first twenty miles or so, after that it's all Ainslie.'

'I see,' she acknowledged quietly, her lips pursing 'Does that mean the head station is a lot larger than the outstation, or just that the homestead is further from the connecting boundary?'

'Both,' he laughed as he bent to retrieve the rifle.

Her curiosity getting the better of her again, Paige looked at him interestedly. 'How large exactly?' she probed.

'What, Ainslie itself, or the whole property, including the outstations?'

Before replying she had another query to make. 'How many outstations are there?'

'Three, but the other two are considerably larger than this one,' he relayed negligently.

'In that case, perhaps you'd better make it the sum total,' she suggested sardonically.

'Then it's a nicely rounded two and a half thousand.' His advice was calmly given.

It obviously wasn't acres or hectares, so what did that leave? 'Square miles or square kilometres?' she speculated, swallowing hard. Either way it sounded an inordinate amount of dirt!

'Miles.'

'Which is how many acres?' She might be able to visualise its size a little better if it was in a measurement she was more familiar with.

His informatve, 'Just over one and a half million,' left her no wiser than before, however, because *that* much land she found it absolutely impossible to envisage!

'And it all belongs to Bruce Morgan?' she questioned faintly.

'In a manner of speaking,' he agreed.

'Meaning?'

'He holds the majority of shares in the company which owns it.'

'It being a private company and the other shareholders being various members of the family, I presume?' ironically.

'It's the usual format with a lot of these large holdings,' Kelly endorsed impassively. 'What's wrong with that?'

'Nothing, I guess ... if you're a member of the family,' she half laughed drily.

'And if you're not?'

'I told you, I don't like monopolies!' she retorted immediately. 'It just doesn't seem right that one person should own so much.'

'That is, not unless the person happens to be one of the Thornton family, eh?' he gibed.

Paige blinked at the sudden hardening of his tone, her expression somewhat bewildered. 'I don't follow you.'

'Greenvale's not exactly what one would call a *small* property either, but I notice its size doesn't appear to have offended you too much!' In a voice heavily laced with sarcasm.

'Only because I didn't know!' she countered earnestly, trying to defend herself.

'And now that you do, what are you going to tell him? That you're not interested in seeing the place any more?'

'Of course not!'

'No, I didn't think you would,' he bit out derisively and, turning his back on her, began leading Mercury away.

Paige watched him go with sombre eyes. Once again he had misconstrued her intentions, but as she already knew from previous experience, there was little to be gained from trying to correct his false impression. He had apparently made up his mind about her and there was nothing she could say or do that was going to make him change it!

CHAPTER FIVE

As she emerged into the hall after her evening shower Paige halted and listened intently to Kelly's voice coming from the spare room. Although she had been at Bindaburra for almost two weeks now this was the first occasion she'd had an opportunity to hear the transceiver being put to use. Every other time Kelly had concluded his report by the time she had finished in the bathroom, but it appeared there was more to discuss tonight than usual.

'It's clearing well this end.' She could hear an unfamiliar voice speaking. 'We managed to make it out to the Round Hill paddock today.'

'Any damage?'

'The fences were down in a couple of places, but they're right again now.' A slight pause and the man added, 'Oh, yes, young Larry succeeded in picking himself up a nice-looking brumby mare and foal on the way. I guess they must have become separated from the rest of the herd when the water rose.'

'Breaking her in will keep him occupied for a while,' Kelly laughed.

A wry grunt and, 'I wish I could find something that would do the same for some of those staying in the homestead.'

'They're giving you trouble?'

'A little. With no races to look forward to now, I think most of them are starting to find the time hanging heavy.'

'Well, why don't you get Suzanne or Michelle to organise a couple of picnics for them? That should get them out of your hair for a time. Now that you can make it to the Hill the Aboriginal rock paintings will keep them occupied for at least one day,' Kelly suggested.

'Good idea!' It was almost possible to see the man's smiling relief. 'How's it going your end, anyway?' he now asked. 'I suppose you'd be starting to cop a bit of flak yourself by now, wouldn't you?'

Since it was obviously a reference to herself Paige moved closer to the doorway, her heart beating erratically as she caught Kelly's deep-throated laugh.

'Not for the conditions, just the company,' he supplied drily.

'At least that's a problem you've a chance of resolving yourself... if you want to,' came the subtle reply. 'What I'd be interested to hear at the moment, though, is when you reckon you'll be back to help untangle mine!'

'Not for another four or five days, probably—I'm sorry, Dave.'

'Hell, as long as that? I expected you to say two at

the most. It's just about clear all the way this end, you know.'

Paige edged nearer still, her interest in the conversation increasing. She had been expecting them to leave very shortly too. As far as she was aware the water had all but disappeared from around Bindaburra too.

'Mmm, but I don't want to begin by having to take detours,' she heard Kelly explain in a significantly ironic tone. 'I'd rather wait and make it in one day if I possibly can.'

'You figure four days there is likely to be less of a headache than two on the track, hmm? was the chuckling return.

'Something like that.'

'Okay then, we'll be . . .'

The remainder of his words were lost as someone began talking in the background and then a girl's voice came winging clearly into the room.

'Kelly, love, you can't possibly mean us to wait another five days for your return, as Dave says, can you?' she queried disbelievingly.

'Sorry, honey, but I'm afraid so,' he sighed. The shared endearments sent an acute stab of misery through Paige. 'You can put up with it for a while longer, can't you?'

'You're not giving me much choice, you brute!' she retorted banteringly. 'But do make it back as quickly as you can, *please*!'

'For you, honey, anything.'

'I think you speak with forked tongue, oh, lying one!' sardonically. 'If what you say is true you wouldn't have gone to Bindaburra in the first place.'

'Someone had to,' he pointed out reasonably.

'But did it really have to be you, at *this* particular time?' she wailed.

'You know the answer to that as well as I do, Suzie.'

'I suppose so,' she conceded with a dramatic sigh. 'It's just that knowing the reason doesn't, unfortunately, always make the result easier to bear.'

'I'm sorry, honey, I really am,' he apologised again. 'I promise I'll make it up to you when I get back, okay?'

'You're too late, *I've* already promised myself that!' A peal of melodious laughter entered the room like a breath of fresh air.

'Witch! What's it going to cost me this time?' And before she could answer, 'No, don't tell me, I think I'd rather not know at the moment.'

'Don't worry, I wasn't going to tell you anyway. It will be my surprise for when you return.'

'I can hardly wait,' drily.

'That's what I thought you'd say,' she gurgled irrepressibly. 'But it's only deserved payment for having left me to ...'

Paige crept quietly away before she could hear any more, and before Kelly could discover her eavesdropping. It really hadn't occurred to her previously that he might have had a girl-friend on Ainslie and the revelation hit her like a bombshell. It didn't take much soul-searching to fathom the reason why it had affected her so greatly either! That first shaft of pain when she heard them talking to each other had been most explicit. She had ridiculously fallen in love with him herself! Hopelessly and incurably in love with someone who not only didn't particularly like her, but whose interest was already centred elsewhere!

Reaching for the packet of cigarettes on the kitchen table, she lit one with shaking fingers and drew on it deeply. Oh, God, how could she have been so stupid not to have realised the direction in which her wayward emotions were propelling her? Not to have known *why* his touch had the power to devastate her nervous system so, and his smile always made her feel so warm and effervescent inside. How could she have been so incredibly naïve? she berated herself despairingly.

Footsteps warned of his approach a few minutes later and she pretended to be absorbed in pouring herself a cup of tea from the pot keeping warm above the stove. When they stopped before reaching the kitchen she realised he had only been heading for the bathroom and his own shower, and she was able to relax slightly. Right at present she didn't feel at all capable of concealing her feelings from his astute gaze.

When he did finally enter the kitchen, dressed in clean denims and a matching shirt, she was considerably more composed although deliberately busy with laying the table.

'What do you fancy for dinner tonight? Anything in particular?' Kelly ran a hand beneath her curling hair to grasp the nape of her neck lightly as he came to stand beside her.

'I don't mind,' she hunched one shoulder disinterestedly, her voice a little throaty. 'Whatever's easiest will do.'

He bent his head slightly so he could view her face more closely. 'No preference at all?' he smiled.

Paige shook her head rapidly and turned away, as if the whole of her attention was required in order to place their cutlery in just the right position. 'No, no preferences.'

Suddenly she was spun around and her face, cupped between two inescapable hands, was tilted upwards. 'Okay, let's have it,' Kelly ordered lazily. 'What have I done now?'

'N-nothing,' she denied jerkily. 'Why should you think you'd done something?' Much less care!

'One, because you're unusually subdued, and two, because you're still refusing to even look at me.'

At that her gaze did flick upwards, involuntarily, but she just as swiftly controlled it again by lowering it to the darkly coloured column of his throat. 'Only because I was looking to see where to put the knives and forks, and—and I'm not subdued, I was thinking, that's all.'

'About what?'

'This and that,' she offered evasively.

'So it has absolutely nothing to do with the conversation you overheard on the transceiver?' he taunted shrewdly.

'How did you know?' The betraying words were out before she could apply a brake to them.

'Does it matter?'

'No.' Paige shook her head selfconsciously, and feeling some sort of apology was called for, added, 'I'm sorry,' in an abashed murmur.

'There's no call to be, you could have spoken to Suzanna if you'd wanted to,' he advised softly, and much to her surprise. 'I expect you're starting to miss the company of your own sex by now. That's one of the things which make it so hard on women out here.'

She hadn't anticipated such consideration, even

though it wasn't strickly necessary. Up until now she had been foolishly content just having him around.

'But you said I wasn't allowed to use the transceiver,' she reminded him, a little perplexed by the sudden reversal.

'No, I said I wouldn't teach you how to work it, not that you couldn't use it while I was here,' he corrected.

It was a fine distinction, but she didn't question it. Instead, she shrugged, 'Oh, well, I probably wouldn't have known what to say to her, anyway.' An understatement if ever there was one! Just what general trivialities did you exchange over the air with the girl-friend of the man you'd fallen in love with?

'Knowing Suzie, I doubt if you'd have been called upon to say anything much ... except provide answers, of course,' Kelly dismissed her excuse drily. 'She's very curious about you.'

So would I be, if I were in her shoes, Paige admitted to herself with an inward grimace. To him, in an attempt to satisfy her own uncontrollable curiosity, she put the question which had been paramount in her mind ever since she had heard the name.

'And—er—just who is Suzanne?'

The corners of his mouth sloped upwards appealingly. 'I thought you would have been able to guess that from our conversation.'

'Yes, I suppose so,' she had little choice but to agree as she stifled a sigh. 'H-have you known her long?'

A deep crease appeared in his forehead and he looked at her strangely. 'For crying out loud, what sort of a question's that to ask?'

'I'm sorry, I didn't realise you'd consider it prying,'

she said, pulling away from him stiffly.

'Prying! Where the hell does prying come into it?'

Paige was becoming totally confused and as a last defence she resorted to indignant anger. 'Well, what else was I supposed to think when you make a reply like that to a query asking if you've known your girl-friend for long?' she demanded huffily.

A slow smile crinkled the corners of Kelly's glittering blue eyes and he started to laugh. 'Suzanne's not my girl-friend, you mixed-up little idiot, she's my sister!'

Fearful that she might have been staring at him open-mouthed, Paige clamped her teeth together force-ably as a bubble of joyous relief exploded inside her —a feeling of happiness which she went to great pains to hide.

'No wonder you thought my remarks were a little peculiar,' she half smiled. 'It just didn't occur to me that your sister might live at Ainslie too.'

Kelly ran a hand around the back of his neck, his laughter becoming tinged with an emotion she couldn't quite define. 'No, I guess it was a logical conclusion to reach from your point of view.'

'Does—does she also work for Mr Morgan?' she enquired shyly.

'Sometimes,' he confirmed laconically. 'Along with keeping my house in order for me.'

'And the man Dave? What does he do?'

'He's an overseer.'

'You don't report to Mr Morgan personally, then?'

'No, Dave does that.' He began reaching for tins from the cupboard.

'I noticed there were no interruptions when you were talking to the homestead. I thought all your calls had to go through a base station,' she probed as she passed him two saucepans.

'Not always,' he disclosed with a shake of his head, then explained, 'With so many transceivers and portables in the network these days the R.F.D.S.—Royal Flying Doctor Service—assigns what are called "chatter frequencies" to certain areas so groups of transceivers can talk between each other informally, but which can be broken into if there's an emergency.'

'Where would your radio base be—Broken Hill?'

'Uh-huh. As the crow flies, about three hundred miles in that direction,' indicating south by south-west.

'And by road?'

'More like five hundred.'

For a moment Paige was silent, imagining. 'It's unbelievable really that people managed to survive at all out here before the days of modern medicines and the aeroplane, isn't it?' she mused.

'A lot of them didn't,' Kelly put in sardonically. 'There's some gruesome tales to be told about the outback. Of operations performed with pocket-knives in the light of hurricane lamps, and people making three or four hundred-mile journeys by horseback and wagon in an effort to reach a doctor in time... and that's *this* century, not the last! Even with modern communications it's still easy to lose your life in this country if you're not continually on your guard. The outback can exhilarate and challenge, or desolate and crush, but one thing it does demand at all times is respect. Forget that, and you do so at your own risk!'

'Don't remind me!' she shivered involuntarily, remembering her own close call. And because she didn't

want to appear overly talkative now that he had informed her of his relationship with Suzanne, she let
the matter drop and assumed a slightly more taciturn
pose for her own protection.

After dinner they played chess, as had become their
custom since Paige discovered Kelly had brought a
travelling set with him, and although she was yet to
win a game—it hadn't taken long for her to realise
he was far too experienced a player for her to van-
quish—she still stuck to it tenaciously, determined to
succeed at least once before they left the outstation.

'It's not fair, you plan too many moves ahead,' she
complained with a smile when, for the third time that
evening, she had been forced to witness her king being
checkmated. 'I had no idea you were planning to
attack through your rook like that.' A mischievous
glance was levelled at him from beneath long curling
lashes and she suggested, 'I don't suppose you'd consider leaving one of your pieces off the board next time,
would you?'

'A pawn?' he quizzed, and she wrinkled her nose at
him wryly.

'No, I had thoughts of your queen, actually!' With
the most capable attacking piece out of the way she
might at least have some chance!

'If I did remove it, would you be happy with a win
under those circumstances?'

Paige sighed. He could read her too well. 'No,' she
admitted ruefully, grimacing. 'But it can't be much of
a challenge for you to keep beating me so easily either.'

'Maybe I find it's worth forgoing the challenge for
the satisfaction,' he proposed, lightly mocking.

Refusing to be drawn by the deliberate taunt, she

sent him a speaking glance from expressive eyes instead. It was bad enough that he was the victor in all their games of chess without giving him the opportunity for another win in a verbal sparring contest as well. She began re-setting the board with renewed purpose. Some time, somehow, she was going to deprive him of that satisfaction!

During the next three days the outstation underwent a startling change as a fresh coat of paint improved its appearance immeasurably, while Kelly covered the bulk of the area with a spray-gun, Paige followed behind applying the contrasting touches to the windows and doors with a roller and a brush. It was the type of work she had often enjoyed helping her father with at home and she had willingly offered her services when she had discovered what Kelly intended for the place.

Now, as she stood back to survey their handiwork gleaming in the late afternoon sunshine, she couldn't help exclaiming, 'Well, it's certainly changed from when I arrived! It looks quite inviting now.'

Kelly looked up from where he was cleaning the equipment they had used, his expression sardonic. 'So much so that you'll be sorry to leave when the time comes, I suppose?' he drawled.

'It's a distinct possibility,' she smiled, still looking at the house consideringly. 'I've grown rather attached to the place since I've been here.'

'Even though it's set in the middle of nowhere?' One well defined eyebrow arched whimsically.

'But that's half its attraction.'

'And the other half?'

'Why, the company, of course!' she grinned facetiously, hiding the state of her true feelings with mockery. 'Who else could have given me such a pleasant and welcoming introduction to the outback?'

'Stuart?' he suggested blandly.

She pretended to give the matter some thought and then moved her head slowly from side to side. 'No, he doesn't have quite your ability to make someone feel *wanted*,' she gibed dulcetly.

'You like to feel ... wanted?' His eyes ranged over her lazily, disconcertingly.

'Well, not quite so *un*wanted,' she modified diffidently. 'There is a happy medium somewhere between the two, you know.'

'But not one we're ever likely to find,' drily.

It was a dispiriting truth to have to accept and Paige did so with a sigh, and what she hoped was a dispassionate shrug of her slender shoulders.

'Maybe not, but I'm still pleased to be able to report that, in spite of your efforts to the contrary, I *do* like it here and you *haven't* managed to turn me off the outback for life!' she tossed at him with a pertly accentuating nod of her head as she turned on her heel and started for the house.

She was towelling herself dry after her shower when she heard Kelly eventually finish for the day and she purposely slowed her movements. It wouldn't hurt him to wait for a while, she decided cheerfully, and even went so far as to turn the shower back on to give her ploy greater credence.

A hand hammering on the door and the shouted instruction, 'Go easy on the water, that might have to last for another year or more!' had her grudgingly turning it off again, however, and pulling a disgruntled

face at the panel which separated them. Why did circumstances always have to support his dictates? He
wasn't really infallible, was he?

When she did finally condescend to leave the bathroom it was to find him waiting for her patiently, one
shoulder leaning against the door-frame of the spare
room almost opposite, hands thrust into the back
pockets of his dark blue denims, and she met his steady
blue-grey gaze with a limpid green innocence.

'I'm so sorry, you should have let me know you
were waiting,' she purred shamelessly.

'As I've been taking my turn in the shower after
you for over two weeks now, I didn't really think it
would be necessary,' he countered ironically.

'Yes, well ... but not usually as early in the day as
this,' she parried, not quite so insouciantly.

On the point of entering the bathroom, he shrugged
lightly. 'I considered it advisable to move everything
forward tonight if we're to get an early start tomorrow.'

'Do you mean ...?' As she spun back to face him the
rest of her question died on her lips as she confronted
a closed door, her expression turning direful. He had
done that on purpose! But not to be routed so effortlessly she merely raised her voice louder and shouted
through the door, 'Do you mean for Ainslie?'

From inside the only sound she could distinguish was
an unconcerned whistle which had her glowering impotently. She would have liked to have done what he
did on her first day there—burst into the room uninvited and demand an answer—but she just wasn't quite
game enough and, as a result, she had no option but
to cool her heels until he chose to re-emerge.

By checking every few minutes to hear when the

shower stopped running she was able to ensure that she was the one lounging casually in the opposite doorway when he did come forth, and although she found it extremely difficult trying to pretend she was unaffected by the fact that his only covering was a towel wrapped about his lean waist, she ignored his mockingly raised brows at finding her still there and pressed on with her queries regardless.

'You did mean we're leaving for Ainslie, didn't you?' she sought verification firstly.

His eyes appeared very blue as they glinted provokingly from within their sooty frames. 'Where else?'

Any number of places probably if she had taken their destination for granted, she decided caustically. 'And when did you make this momentous decision? As you walked into the bathroom?'

'No, I've been weighing the pros and cons for most of the day, as a matter of fact,' Kelly revealed as he continued down the hall.

Paige followed him swiftly to the bedroom, pulling a face at the rippling muscles of his back as she went. 'You might at least have let me know,' she censured resentfully.

He grinned at her indignant expression. 'There didn't seem much point until I'd actually made my decision.'

'In other words, I wasn't important enough to warrant consultation!'

'As you're knowledge of the route we'll be taking is absolutely zero, there wasn't anything you could contribute,' he shrugged indolently.

'Except for one small thing . . . an interest in those arrangements which happen to concern *me*!' she railed.

'Or isn't that allowed when the arbitrary Kelly Sinclair's in charge?'

The gibing words were hardly out before long fingers had ensnarled her chin and his head bent closer. 'Don't try pushing me too hard, Paige Darling, or I could be tempted to return the favour... with disastrous results!'

'For whom?' she dared to challenge defiantly.

Kelly's well-shaped mouth widened into a heart-stopping smile which had her going weak at the knees. 'Now there's a superfluous question if ever I've heard one,' he drawled. 'Who do you think I meant?'

It was difficult to appear confident with his lips so near hers and she shifted restively from one foot to the other. 'There's a big gap between meaning and achieving,' she retaliated somewhat breathlessly.

'Want to bet?'

The dancing light in his eyes warned Paige it was wiser not to attempt an answer to that goading invitation and she returned to her original complaint instead.

'I still don't think it would've hurt you to have discussed the matter with me,' she pouted.

'Okay, we'll talk about it over dinner,' Kelly grinned ruefully, releasing her. 'Now, make yourself scarce while I get dressed,' turning her around and propelling her peremptorily towards the door.

'It's my bedroom too!' she protested fractiously, piqued at being so perfunctorily dismissed. But when a flexing of wide shoulders indicated his complete indifference as to whether she stayed or left and he moved to discard the towel, she judiciously traded perversity for propriety and fled anyway.

Their meal that night was, of necessity, something of a scratch affair. This was due to the fact that the contents of the small fridge had to be used in order to leave it empty when the generator was turned off. Nevertheless, as all the ingredients seemed to complement each other well enough it was still a tasty repast and they consumed it appreciatively.

'What time will we be leaving?' Paige asked as she disposed of the last of the cheese and began carrying the plates to the sink.

'First light,' Kelly relayed drily.

She gave an instinctive shudder and grimaced. 'It'll be cold.'

'Mmm, so you'd best make certain you take something warm with you.'

She slanted him an extremely wry glance. 'Such as?'

'I get your meaning,' he laughed, and rose to his feet. 'I'll hunt out a jacket or something for you before I forget.'

While he was gone Paige set to work on their few dishes and was almost finished by the time he returned.

'I've left a sweater on the chair for you,' he nodded back towards the bedroom.

'Thank you.' And, curiously, 'Will you be taking all your gear back with you?'

'Some—most of it will stay here, though. Besides, I want to travel as lightly as possible anyway, just in case we strike a few bad patches.'

'I see.' She turned away to concentrate on what she was doing. 'So you're not anticipating staying at Ainslie for very long, after all?'

He shrugged but didn't give a definite answer as he began making the coffee and, consequently, she had no recourse but to let that particular subject lapse.

'What will you do with Mercury? Leave him here too?' she asked next.

'That's right,' he nodded. 'I brought him across by float originally, but there's no way we could tow that behind us tomorrow. He'll be fine for a few days in the yard until someone either comes back to stay, or else collects him. There's plenty of shade, feed and water.'

Thoughtfully, she started to dry the plates she had washed and put them away. 'Have you advised the—er —homestead that we're leaving in the morning?'

'Of course.' The mocking curve of his mouth became decidedly more pronounced. 'We can't all wander around the outback as the whim takes us without telling anyone our intended route or our E.T.A.'

Disregarding the pointed gibe, Paige looked across at him contemplatively. 'And what did they say?'

'Who, the homestead?' he queried in surprise, and after her confirming nod, 'Have a good trip. I hope we'll see you some time tomorrow afternoon. What did you expect them to say?'

'I don't really know,' she half smiled selfconsciously. For some unaccountable reason she felt apprehensive about her move to Ainslie. Perhaps, because she would be an uninvited guest amongst total strangers. 'I just thought they might have—might have . . .'

'Mentioned you?'

'Yes,' she admitted uncomfortably, and immediately dropped her gaze.

With his hands resting on drill-clad hips, Kelly eyed her consideringly. 'You're not still worried about having to stay there, are you?'

'A little,' she smiled again, but with even more discomfort this time.

'For heaven's sake, why?' He stared at her uncomprehendingly. 'I thought we'd settled all this last time.'

'So did I,' she owned with a half laugh. 'But I can't help the way I feel. I'm just not looking forward to it, that's all.'

'Because you don't like monopolies ... or those who control them?'

'Maybe.' She hunched one shoulder moodily. 'And maybe because I know I have absolutely nothing in common with people like that.'

'But you do have with Stuart and Greenvale!'

If nothing else, the roughly spoken taunt served to put things back into perspective. 'I suppose the situations aren't so very different, are they?' she sighed musingly.

'And it's only taken you two and a half weeks to recognise the fact,' he retorted ironically.

'Okay, okay, perhaps I am seeing problems where none exist,' she allowed ruefully. 'From now on I promise I'll try and reserve judgment until I've met your boss for myself. He will be there, I take it? He's not a Pitt Street farmer.'

Kelly's lips twitched humorously. 'No, he is not an absentee owner, and yes, he will be there.'

The last of the pots was returned to the cupboard and she draped the tea towel over the rack above the stove. 'Together with his family?' she asked.

'And guests.'

'Guests?' she echoed, frowning.

'You're not the only one who anticipated attending the races and ball, and ended up by being stranded instead,' he divulged sardonically.

'Oh?' Her face cleared quickly. 'Is that who you meant the other night on the transceiver when you suggested taking them for picnics?'

'That's them,' he nodded, and began pouring the coffee.

Paige accepted the cup he passed to her and added sugar slowly. 'How many are there?'

'Too many, by the sound of what Suzanne had to say,' he laughed.

'Didn't they realise the place was going to be cut off so completely either?'

'Oh, they knew all right, and quite a few did leave while they still had the chance, but the rest...' he shrugged and sat down opposite her at the table. 'Well, I gather they thought it would be a fun experience with which to regale the other members of their social set when they returned to town.'

'Only now they're not finding it quite so amusing.'

'That's about the size of it.' He stretched across to the dresser behind him and picked up the chess set and board. 'Feel like trying your luck one last time before we leave?' he enquired with a teasing look.

Paige wrinkled her nose at him with mock resentment. 'Stop making it sound as if you know the result already. Of course I want another try!'

And another, and another, she noted with increasing exasperation as the evening wore on. Just because it was their last night he obviously wasn't intending to take it easy on her and give anything away! She seemed to be able to hold her own against him for just so long and then... And *then* he always managed to get that one opening he was looking for and from there on it was utter defeat as far as she was concerned.

'One more!' she pleaded earnestly as Kelly checked with his watch after her third loss. 'I think I'm just getting wise to your method of play.'

'Thanks for the warning,' he drawled lazily. 'So what happens if I decide to change my style?'

Paige leant back in her chair and sent him an impish grin. 'Well, that's one of the beauties of being a loser, you see. My play can only improve, because it just isn't possible to get any worse!'

'Okay, one more,' Kelly relented, amused.

Fervently determined that she was going to make amends for all her previous defeats and that this would be the game whereby she turned the tables on him, Paige refused to let her concentration wander for even a minute and studied each move from every angle possible before committing any of her pieces. And for a time it looked as if she might even have been getting the upper hand, but when he skilfully repulsed her latest attack and put her squarely on the defensive in return, she knew beyond a doubt that nothing had changed. No matter which way he played she just couldn't find the necessary strategies to beat him. That was, unless...

Unless that bishop which was causing so much of her trouble could be discreetly removed from its menacing position! She drew in her breath deeply struggling hard to contain the outrageous grin she could feel pulling at her lips. What she was contemplating wasn't fair and it wasn't honourable, but by hook or by crook, she *was* going to win *one* game, she promised herself gleefully.

Her opportunity presented itself sooner than she

had hoped—before she had lost too many of her own men—and when Kelly left the table in order to fetch another packet of cigarettes she surreptitiously nudged the offending piece on to the adjacent square. It wasn't an immediately noticeable move, but it did make a tremendous amount of difference to her play, as witnessed by the prompt capture of one of his knights.

For her next couple of moves Paige was content to simply consolidate her improved position, but her following move was halted almost before it had begun.

'H-o-l-d it!' Her wrist was encircled by firm fingers and held away from the board. 'There's something very peculiar going on here.'

'Because you're not winning as effortlessly as you thought you would?' she taunted daringly.

'Because that's one piece you shouldn't be able to move,' he corrected softly.

'Why not?' She opened her eyes artlessly wide. 'There's nothing to stop me.'

His eyes sought her face watchfully. 'Which is exactly where the peculiarity occurs ... because there should be.'

'But there isn't,' she smiled sunnily.

'I know,' he agreed so silkily that she had to drop her gaze. 'So let's just check back over a few moves, shall we?'

What could she say? 'If you want.'

'Well! Will you look at that?' he exclaimed drily a few seconds later. 'Both my bishops are on white squares. No wonder you were able to take that last piece without loss!'

Paige had to bite down on her lip to stop a broad smile from showing. 'Maybe you set them up incor-

rectly when we started the game,' she offered helpfully.

'In which case, I wouldn't have been able to keep
your queen out of the play for so long, would I?'

'Wouldn't you?' It was becoming almost impossible
not to laugh. 'I—er—hadn't noticed.'

'Too busy working out moves for both of us, hmm?'

Her eyes sparkled emerald green from beneath the
cover of luxuriantly long lashes. 'Goodness, what a
terrible thing to say!' she chided. 'You know, if you
don't like being beaten then you really shouldn't play
the game.'

'Neither should anyone who's not prepared to take
their medicine when they're caught trying to put one
over,' he countered just as mockingly.

'You surely can't be referring to me!' she gasped.

'Oh, no?' Blue eyes held hers tauntingly as he gained
his feet and seemed to tower over the table. 'We'll
just see about that, won't we, my equivocating little
cheat?'

Jumping to her own feet, Paige pulled backwards,
breaking his grip, her lips pouting provocatively.
'Heavens, I don't know what all the fuss is about, it
was only such a little move. I thought you'd be able
to overcome that tiny setback without any trouble at
all.'

He began moving slowly, deliberately, around the
table. 'And maybe I will ... once I've squared our
account.'

'But I was only trying to make the game more of a
challenge for you,' she laughed excusingly while putting more distance between them. 'Or can't you take
a joke?'

'I certainly hope *you* can, because I assure you, I'll be the one who's laughing last,' he threatened a retaliation which sent an uncontrollable quiver of nervous excitement along her veins and had her skipping still further away.

'Now, Kelly, don't do anything you might come to regret,' she exhorted with persuasive audacity. 'I mean —be honest—you couldn't really expect me to let you win every game we played, now could you?'

His teeth shone whitely in a wide smile and every trace of indolence suddenly left his stance. 'Don't worry, Rusty, regret isn't likely to enter into it. At least, not as far as I'm concerned,' he forecast provokingly.

'Well, if that's the kind of mood you're in, I think I might just take myself off for a last walk around the place and come back when you're in a better frame of mind!' she proposed facetiously as she flung open the door and whirled out on to the verandah.

'Oh, no, you don't!'

Paige shrieked, partly with trepidation and partly with laughter, when she saw him lunge after her and, clearing the steps with a flying leap, she raced around the corner of the building and flew for the concealing darkness beyond the range of the lights beaming through the windows, thankful that as the water had disappeared so had most of the mosquitoes.

Expecting him to catch her at any moment, she dodged behind the first tree she came to, fully prepared to have to evade his reach when he followed her. But as she spun to face the way she had come the only sound to break the waiting silence was her own heavy breathing and she glanced about her warily. A few more minutes spent peering at the surrounding moonlit trees and searching the clearing convinced her that she was safe for the moment and she relaxed visibly. At least it gave her a chance to regain her breath and to recover some of her equanimity.

The air was abruptly rent by a cow calling plaintively to its calf, followed closely by a sharp rustle in the scrub at her back and, momentarily reliving the moment when the scrubber had burst into view in front of her, she swivelled around in heart-pounding alarm. Such was her relief at finding Kelly confronting her and not some maddened bull that she completely forgot the reason for her being where she was and slid down into a squatting position with her back against the tree, a sigh of pure thankfulness escaping her lips.

'Thank heavens it's only you! I had visions of that damned bull coming back to have another go at me,' she grinned.

'From the grave?' quizzically.

'Not exactly, but one just like it,' she laughed.

'He did put a scare into you, didn't he?' Kelly remarked wryly as he leant over to help her to her feet.

'Of course he did!' she exclaimed spiritedly, then went on to quip, 'Bullfighting wasn't part of the curriculum at the school I attended.'

'But man-baiting was, I presume?'

Trapped between him and the tree, Paige flicked the tip of her tongue over suddenly dry lips and eyed him doubtfully. 'Wh-what makes you say that?'

'You do it so effectively,' he drawled softly.

'I—er—that's ...' She tried to think of a flippant retort, but she was so occupied in attempting to overcome the feeling of drowning in the glittering blue sea of his eyes that her mental processes just weren't functioning as she could have wished.

When one encircling arm drew her firmly to his rugged frame and a gentle hand smoothed its way along the side of her neck to tangle in her curly hair she could only melt against him acquiescently, her soft lips parting, warm and responsive beneath his stimulating mouth as it moved over hers.

She was oblivious to everything but the man who was holding her so possessively. The clean male smell of him; the feel of his hard muscular body strained against hers; the pleasantly fresh taste of him; and the touch which had her senses flaming into scorching, searing life when an exploring hand sought and found the satiny bare skin beneath her flowing blouse to caress the swelling contours of a rounded breast and bring a moan of desire and pleasure to her throat.

Of their own free will her arms curved about his neck as she arched invitingly closer, her emotions aroused to a tumultuous fever pitch she hadn't believed possible by his sensuous touch, and her mind unconsciously subduing the wish to hear him say her love was returned when his increasing ardour kindled even more fervent responses.

Then, without warning, he was stepping backwards and dragging her arms from around his neck, his breathing harsh and uneven in the electrically charged silence as an extinguishing grey prevailed over the intense blue in his eyes and the set of his mouth tautened savagely.

'Dear God, I think it's just as well we're leaving in the morning,' he rasped grimly. 'I can see this situation having some very regrettable consequences if we're not careful. So I suggest you head for the house, right now, and leave me to ensure I've got everything we require for the journey tomorrow.'

Which all too clearly showed Paige, to her aching despair, that it had only been a momentary lapse in his self-control due to their circumstances which had prompted his advances, but rather than allow him to guess just how deeply involved her feelings were she gave an uncaring shrug and nodded.

'You're quite right, of course,' she agreed with what she prayed was the right amount of indifference. But just in case it wasn't enough, 'It's strange how two people can become physically attracted—against their inclinations—when they're thrown together for a length of time, isn't it?'

A muscle rippled spasmodically, conspicuously, beside Kelly's chiselled jaw and then disappeared. 'Very!' he snapped succinctly.

Paige swallowed hard, pretending his terse agreement left her unaffected, and began humming with feigned nonchalance as she sauntered towards the house. It was the only way she could think to sustain her flagging spirits and disguise the state of her churning emotions.

CHAPTER SIX

A HAND on her shoulder had Paige opening her eyes and staring drowsily upwards as Kelly bent over her.

'What time is it?' she asked sleepily.

'Almost time we left.'

'Oh, that's right, we're going to Ainslie today, aren't we?' She had forgotten for a moment, but now it came flooding back and she pushed herself into a sitting position. His pillow, she noticed, was as smooth and untouched as when she had gone to bed the previous evening and she queried frowningly, 'Didn't you get to bed at all last night?'

His mouth curved crookedly. 'Not in here.'

'Then where?' Who knew better than she that it wasn't possible to make one up elsewhere?

'It doesn't matter, I managed,' he brushed her question aside repressively. 'Breakfast's ready whenever you are.'

'Okay, it won't take me a minute to get dressed,' she half smiled, unsure of his mood. 'And it's not as if I have much to pack.'

'I wasn't aware you had *anything* to pack,' he commented wryly.

She grinned and indicated her nightdress as an example. 'You're forgetting these. I shall still need something other than just my slacks and top if I'm going to be there for some time.'

'Suzanne should be able to provide you with something a little more fashionable. You'd be much the same size.'

'Maybe,' she granted. 'But I think I'll take them along anyway. They're very comfortable.' And they were a memento of her stay at Bindaburra!

'As you like.' He turned to leave. 'Don't be long, though, I'd prefer to get away as soon as possible.'

The first pearl grey streaks of dawn were just rising above the horizon to chase away the ebony shadows of night when they left the outstation, and craning her head over her shoulder for one last look Paige sighed softly, disconsolately, when the house was finally lost to view amid the surrounding trees. It would always hold a rather special place in her affections.

It wasn't until they had completed almost an hour's travel and dawn's half light gave way to brilliant day that she was really able to see much of the country they were covering. It was a magnificent sight as the early sun bathed the landscape with a sparkling radiance which brought every colour of the rainbow vividly to life as it struck and was reflected back from sandstone rocks, earth, trees, and sky. Occasionally they passed small pools of water, not yet evaporated by the sun but diminishing quickly, and although the ground was still obviously very soft beneath the Land Cruiser's wheels they were managing to make reasonably good progress.

Here and there they could see small groups of cattle which had made their way down from the plateau as the waters receded. Now they grazed placidly on the fresh green shoots which were springing tall in the sunlight, along with a colourful array of wildflowers, while in the distance a family of kangaroos scratched out hollows in the soil for themselves beneath a couple of coolibahs so they could doze peacefully through the hottest part of the day before foraging for food again at dusk.

After coming to a corner post where four paddocks joined, each with a wide steel connecting gate, they drove through to the one diagonally opposite. It soon became apparent, even to Paige, that the vehicle was finding it much harder going as their route gradually became more waterlogged, and she wasn't at all surprised to hear Kelly mutter an imprecation under his breath shortly afterwards and radically change direction.

'One of the detours you predicted might be necessary?' she quizzed ruefully.

'Mmm,' he nodded without looking at her, but concentrating on choosing the most suitable course. 'I was hoping not to strike trouble until we'd made it to those rocks up ahead. Now it looks as if we'll have to skirt the whole damned lot of it.'

'Move into another paddock, you mean?'

'No, I doubt it will come to that,' he replied evenly. 'We've got twenty-five thousand acres to play with.'

'As much as that?' Paige looked out of the window with new interest. 'It must take a while to muster it.'

'About a week by three or four men on horseback. A lot less by plane,' he volunteered.

She turned in her seat to face him. 'Is there much mustering done by air?'

'More and more,' Kelly disclosed finally when they had gained the top of a small rocky incline. 'It saves a tremendous amount of time when you have large areas to cover.'

'Yes, I suppose it would,' she conceded. 'What sort of a plane do they use, a helicopter?'

'Usually.' His head dipped in acknowledgment.

'Hired?'

'Some hire, some buy,' he shrugged casually. 'It all depends on the economics of each individual situation.'

Leaning far back in her seat now, Paige sent him a wry sideways glance. 'But Bruce Morgan owns.'

'Is that a question, or one of those considered opinions of yours?' he countered, his tone one degree less tolerant.

'Call it an intuitive guess,' she suggested pertly. 'He does own one, though, doesn't he?'

'Not personally,' he divulged with quite a bite to his voice this time. 'It was purchased by the company, for the company.'

'And he, coincidentally, just happens to *be* the company,' she goaded recklessly. Then, before he could retaliate in a manner she also intuitively guessed was coming, she held up her hands in a gesture of surrender. 'Okay, okay, don't tear me to pieces, I was only having you on! He can have twenty helicopters for all I care.'

Fleetingly, she was raked by a pair of sardonic grey eyes. 'He'll be grateful for your approval, I'm sure.'

'I'm sure he will be too,' she grimaced drily. '*If* he accidentally notices I'm alive.'

'Meaning?'

'Only that people who own over a million acres of land no doubt have an equivalent amount of dollars to go with it! And as I, unfortunately,' she sighed with mock dolefulness, 'have not yet reached that pinnacle of opulence, then apart from a brief introduction, he's hardly likely to single me out as worthy of his recognition ... except as an idiot and a nuisance for having become stranded on one of his properties!'

'On Ainslie that only makes you one of many at the moment,' he drawled, irony predominant.

Her return glance was wry. 'Thanks! You really know how to make a person feel good, don't you?'

'I thought I was consoling you, making you feel more like one of the crowd, as it were,' he returned, a mocking curve sweeping across his shapely mouth.

Paige made a moue of vexed exasperation but didn't reply. All her attention was abruptly needed to avoid being thrown bruisingly against the door because in order to gain better traction for the Land Cruiser they were having to follow a much rougher path, and nor was the noise as they jarred and jolted their way around the lower lying land particularly conducive to conversation.

All too thankful when Kelly eventually brought them to a halt for lunch, she alighted slowly, easing circulation back into aching muscles and limbs she was positive would never recover from the buffeting they had received and squinted into the heat-blurred distance.

'Have we passed the halfway point yet?' She looked back with bated breath to where he was making a fire so they could boil some of the water they carried for tea. She didn't think she could stand it if he said they hadn't!

'Just about,' he smiled, his teeth very white against his mahogany-coloured skin. 'Why, had enough?'

'Haven't you?' she retorted instead of answering. 'No one, not even you, could possibly enjoy driving over the sort of terrain we've just covered.'

'No, it's a pretty tough route, this one,' he averred. 'But it should improve from now on, the worst is behind us.'

'Thank the lord for that!' She heaved a grateful sigh and sank back sideways on to the passenger seat, her feet resting on the ground outside. 'I wouldn't want to be too stiff to move when I arrive at Ainslie, as well.'

'That's right, you didn't really take to our other method of ground travel either, did you?' he grinned in remembrance. 'As I've said before, you should have stayed in the city where you know what it's all about, Rusty.'

'And as I've said before, don't call me Rusty!' she flared, annoyed with herself for letting his remark upset her. 'I don't like nicknames.'

'Another reason you shouldn't have come outback?' He fixed her with a questioning look. 'There's very few who don't have one out here.'

'Oh, and what's your ... Flint?' she quipped.

Kelly's ensuing burst of laughter had waves of unbelievable attraction swamping her nervous system. 'You figure that could be why we strike sparks off each other?' he drawled.

It was impossible for her to fight his appeal and her own amusement at the same time and a grudging grin finally made an appearance. 'More than likely,' she concurred ruefully. And because she was afraid the way she felt about him was too apparent in her eyes she made a show of looking into the back of the vehicle and asking, 'Is there—er—anything else you want from in here?'

*

There were two creeks which had to be crossed during the afternoon and although one was over three feet deep they were both forded without difficulty by what Kelly informed her was the standard practice of re- moving the fanbelt—not only to stop the water being churned up, but also to stop the fan from slowing the engine—and tying a sheet of canvas across the radi- ator grille. This latter precaution causing a bubble of air to form beneath the bonnet, as well as preventing the water from flooding into the engine as he drove steadily through in low gear.

After that there were no more obstacles to be over- come and the travelling became progressively easier as they continued on—and on, and on, Paige added to herself—their way. Even so, it was still very late in the afternoon before Kelly could point out a cluster of buildings in the distance and, hot and tired though she was, she combed her fingers quickly through her hair in an attempt to give it some semblance of tidiness and waited impatiently, albeit a little nervously, for a closer view.

As they were moving across country and not using the normal road from town their approach was by way of the rear of the station, and after thumping over a wide cattle grid Kelly began indicating the numerous and various outbuildings, and their particular uses, as they made their way around what Paige could only describe as a small township.

When the homestead itself became visible, set some distance apart from the rest of the buildings amid its own immaculately tended gardens and lawns and surrounded by a white park fence, she drew in a long slow breath and surveyed it sardonically. No less sumptuous than she had anticipated, it was wide and low, with of course those necessary shading verandahs encircling the whole structure, and which was, she realised as they continued on to the front entrance, built in the form of an H.

Between the two front wings was a partially flagstoned courtyard, complete with fountain, formal garden beds, and a gracefully weeping pepper tree to complement the blaze of colour created by the flowering creepers which draped themselves over the trellised verandah railings and step supports, where a number of people were beginning to congregate.

A tall, brown-haired woman, extremely smartly dressed, was the first to detach herself from the crowd and, feeling somewhat like the star attraction for the circus, Paige stepped selfconsciously out of the Land Cruiser and ran her hands down the sides of her slacks as she shortened the woman's walk by a couple of paces.

'Paige, isn't it?' The enquiry was accompanied by a pleasantly welcoming smile. 'I hope you don't mind me calling you that, but since you've been at Bindaburra all this time I really feel as if I already know you. I'm Michelle Morgan-Sinclair.'

There was no time for anything more than the briefest of responses, coupled with a slightly perplexed frown over the name, before another two young women had come to join them. One, in her mid-twenties with lustrous dark hair, soft brown eyes, and a ready smile; and the other closer to thirty, her cool blonde looks enhanced by the faultless cut and expensive material of her casual clothing, but whose attention seemed drawn to Kelly as he leant back against the vehicle to watch the proceedings with alert eyes rather than to the latest guest.

'This is my daughter Suzanne,' Michelle Morgan-Sinclair continued immediately, indicating the younger of the two beside her, 'and this . . .'

'I'm Nadine Morgan-Sinclair, Kelly's wife!' the blonde interrupted, choosing to introduce herself proprietorially, and not a little smugly.

'Ex!'

Who added that amending prefix Paige neither knew nor cared. Her every emotion was shrinking from the cold, hard rock of suspicion which had settled suffocatingly on her chest and was threatening to choke her with the dreaded thought of what those names revealed. She felt like crying and sobbing aloud her bewilderment and hurt, but she didn't, she listened to Michelle's introductions to the rest of those present who now milled around them, and although she made a reply each time, what was actually said—either to or by her—failed completely to register on her mind.

Her reflexes might have been operating automatically, but it seemed her brain was functioning solely for the purpose of increasing her despair and humiliation by recalling all those incidences which were beginning to take on such entirely different connotations. Kelly's teasing about her wanting a job; the laughingly proffered invitation to the homestead—his amusement obviously directed at her—and which she had innocently said he wasn't in a position to offer; his quick defence of the owner of Ainslie; and his humorous denial of her suggestion that his wife's lavish entertaining might have put him in the poor house! Oh, God! How childishly gullible she had been, and how utterly diverting he must have found it all!

At last the introductions were completed and she could stop forcing a smile on to lips which wanted to do anything but. Some of the guests were already wandering back towards the house, out of the hot sun, but before Michelle could bid her to do likewise Paige about-faced swiftly, her eyes searching out Kelly as he stood talking to Nadine.

Perhaps his eyes had been focussed on her too—she didn't know—but immediately her gaze came to rest on him he began closing the gap between them and, in that single instant, all her lacerated emotions crystallised into a protectively white hot and seething fury.

'Kelly *Bruce Morgan*-Sinclair?' she sought the final, incontrovertible proof of his duplicity in bitter tones.

His head inclined acknowledgingly, mockingly, it seemed to her. 'At your service,' he owned levelly.

'You devil!'

This time she made no mistake and her open hand cracked across his cheek before he had a chance to block it, the sound slicing through the air like a burst of gunfire and making them the cynosure of all inquisitive eyes.

'Well, that's gratitude for you, I must say!'

Nadine's shocked voice overrode a few less outspoken comments, but there was only one reaction Paige was waiting for and she shivered apprehensively, in spite of her anger, at the thought of the iron self-control Kelly was imposing on himself breaking. It was an unforgivable thing to have done with everyone there to witness it, but it had been an instinctive retaliation on her part, the only way in which she could avenge, at least to some small degree, the raw and aching misery his deception had created.

Now, as he bent his head threateningly closer, she

could feel her nerves stretching to such an extent that it was only through sheer willpower she made herself stand and face him.

'You ever try a stunt like that again, Paige, and I'll be returning the compliment in kind, so don't say you haven't been warned!' he ground out savagely before brushing past her and heading for the homestead.

All things considered, Paige supposed she had escaped lightly, but unfortunately that didn't stop her from shaking with emotion, nor did it halt the flow of tears to her eyes, and if it hadn't been for Suzanne's comforting presence she doubted whether she would have had the courage to look any of them in the face again.

'Well, I don't profess to know what that was all about, but you certainly added a little spice to what has otherwise been a very uneventful day,' the dark-haired girl with the pixie smile remarked incorrigibly as she put a supporting arm around Paige's waist to begin escorting her inside. 'You've also managed to do the impossible—which is to put Michelle in a quan-dary. She doesn't know now whether she ought to continue playing the gracious hostess, or rush off in motherly outrage after her son and find out what the hell is going on.'

'No, I suppose I haven't exactly endeared myself to her, have I?' Paige brooded wanly, and in an effort to distract her thoughts, 'Do you always call your mother by her first name?'

'Mmm, everyone does,' came the cheerful confirma-tion. 'As far back as I can remember she's always been Michelle, never Mrs Morgan-Sinclair, so as the years passed we just followed suit. You'll be expected to do the same too while you're here.'

'After the exhibition I just put on she may prefer something more formal where I'm concerned.'

'Don't be silly, of course she won't! You may have caught her by surprise for a moment, but she realises it's not likely you did it solely to make a scene. If she thought you had, she wouldn't still be outside,' Suzanne assured her confidently, indicating to where her mother waited for them to join her.

Nevertheless, an apology was called for and Paige wasted no time in offering one immediately they came abreast of the older woman.

'I'm very sorry, Mrs Morgan-Sinclair,' no matter what Suzanne said to the contrary it was impossible for her to use a more familiar mode of address under the circumstances, 'my behaviour was inexcusable,' she murmured contritely, sincerely. 'I had no right to subject everyone to such an embarrassing display.'

'Yes, well, our emotions do get the better of all of us at some time or another,' Michelle smoothed tactfully over the incident. 'So I suggest we say no more about it and, let's hope, by tomorrow everyone will have forgotten it ever happened.'

Except for Kelly, surmised Paige miserably, even as she sent his mother a grateful smile. Somehow, and not that she could really blame him, she couldn't picture him being quite as tolerant, or forgiving, as his parent!

'And do call me Michelle.' Paige suddenly realised she was being spoken to again as they moved across the courtyard towards the steps. 'I think it's so much more friendly to use christian names, don't you?'

'Yes—and thank you,' she smiled, her distress not quite so noticeable now.

'Didn't I tell you?' Suzanne sent one eyebrow quirking ceilingwards a few minutes later after they had left her mother at the wide wainscoted entrance hall while they continued down the passageway to the gold and white decorated room Paige was to use. 'No one calls Michelle by her full name.'

'She's very kind,' Paige reflected quietly, glancing around the elegantly appointed room in silent, though somewhat self-mocking, appreciation. 'There aren't many who would be so understanding when confronted by such bad manners from a perfect stranger.'

The older girl sank down on to the bed and eyed her keenly from beneath long lashes. 'Well, one does have to assume that Kelly isn't altogether without blame, and that you weren't trying to knock his head off his shoulders just for the fun of it,' she quipped drily. 'You *did* have a reason, I gather?'

'Oh, yes!' Paige nodded bitterly, hugging her arms about herself. 'You see, he conveniently forgot to tell me who he was!' she relayed, feeling some sort of explanation was owed.

Suzanne's wide-eyed expression mirrored her incredulity. 'You mean, in all the time you spent at Bindaburra, you never knew his name?'

'Only as Kelly Sinclair—not as Kelly Morgan-Sinclair, the owner of the whole damned shooting match! *That* I didn't discover until your mother began making introductions this afternoon.'

'And was it really such a terrible revelation?'

Paige's head lifted a trifle defiantly. She should have known his family wouldn't appreciate the significance the withholding of his full name held for her.

'Yes, it was, as a matter of fact,' she announced stiffly. 'It's not a very pleasant experience finding you've been lied to, laughed at, and deliberately misled for nearly three weeks.'

'No, I don't suppose it would be,' Suzanne owned sincerely. 'Although I wasn't meaning to be critical, you know ... only curious.' Her head tilted to one side questioning, two puzzled creases appearing between her brows. 'You really believe it was an error of commission rather than omission, and that he purposely set out to deceive you?'

'I know he did!'

'But for what purpose? What did he hope to gain?'

'Who knows? Maybe he just has a warped sense of humour,' Paige half laughed hollowly.

'But it's so unlike him!' Suzanne protested. 'I know Kelly can be high-handed, caustic, and even plain ruthless on occasion, but he certainly isn't malicious!'

As one slender shoulder rose upwards so the corners of Paige's curving mouth took a downward turn. 'Perhaps I bring out the worst in him.'

The older girl's impish smile came to the fore again. 'I find that hard to believe. You don't look the type to incur disfavour with the opposite sex to me.'

'One man's meat is another man's poison,' came the mocking rejoinder.

'Hmm, and sometimes we can't see the wood for the trees either!' Suzanne quoted in turn.

'Meaning?'

'That I can't quite rid myself of the feeling that there's more to this than meets the eye.'

Paige shrugged. It wasn't an assumption she could go along with, but if Kelly's sister wanted to then that was her prerogative, and understandable. Meanwhile, however, the conversation was only serving to keep the painful and tormenting memories fresh in her mind, and she swiftly took the opportunity the ensuing lull provided to propel Suzanne's thoughts elsewhere.

'I guess you'll be glad when the water's disappeared altogether... and us along with it,' she remarked drily.

'Well, I certainly won't be shedding any tears to see some of Nadine's companions bicker their way over the horizon, that's for sure,' Suzanne laughed. 'But I'll miss Michelle when she leaves, as usual.'

Paige's glance was one of surprise. 'Doesn't your mother live here with you, then?'

'Not since Dad died about six years ago,' Suzanne explained, shaking her head. 'She has an apartment in Adelaide these days where she likes to keep her finger on the pulse of things. Oh, she always comes back here whenever there's anything on—birthdays, Christmas, the Races and Ball, that sort of thing—but mostly she stays in town.'

'Don't you mind?'

'In a resentful sense, you mean?' Suzanne queried, and without waiting for a reply, smiled equably, 'Not in the slightest. Kelly and I figure she's just as entitled to live where she chooses as we are, so now she lives there with our blessing and we stay here with hers, and that keeps everyone happy. Besides, I rather think Ainslie holds a few too many memories for her to be entirely happy here any more,' she added musingly.

'So now you run the homestead instead,' Paige put in quickly, distractingly.

'But not nearly so efficiently,' Suzanne grinned, clapping a hand to her forehead and rising hurriedly to her feet. 'To wit, it completely slipped my mind this morning to warn our housekeeper that there would be another two for dinner this evening. If I leave it any later she'll probably resign on the spot!' At the door she paused and looked back. 'Oh, a word of friendly advice ... make sure you're wearing your Sunday best tonight, won't you? I've a sneaking suspicion Nadine means to put us all in the shade now that Kelly's home, and we don't want to be eclipsed, do we?' with a wink.

'I'm afraid I am already wearing my Sunday best,' Paige advised ruefully as she glanced down at her slacks and top.

'Of course! How stupid of me to have forgotten that too!' Suzanne shook her head in despair. 'Well, I'll tell you what, you have a nice leisurely bath or shower, or whatever—I expect you're looking forward to one after your trip today—then when I come back we can sort out some clothes for you. Okay?'

'Fine, thank you,' Paige smiled diffidently. 'As long as it's no trouble.'

'Don't be an idiot, it's my pleasure,' was the laughing admonishment as the other girl left.

In order to keep her thoughts from straying into areas she would rather they didn't go, Paige did as Suzanne had suggested and took a long invigorating shower in the adjoining white and gold bathroom, luxuriating in the use of the toiletries provided and which she had had to do without during her stay at the outstation. It was wonderfully refreshing to be able to work shampoo and conditioner into her hair again and to pamper her fine-textured skin with creams, cologne, and powder, so that by the time she re-entered her bedroom, clad in a fluffy white bathrobe, she felt almost a new person.

A few minutes later, on answering a knock at her

door, she found a smiling Suzanne outside. 'I've managed to save the day,' she was informed cheerfully as an inviting hand was stretched towards the room across the hall. 'Now, shall we proceed?'

'After you,' she smiled back, and followed the other girl into the largest bedroom she had ever seen outside the movies, and where modern built-in furniture made it appear even more extensive but did nothing to detract from the gracious old-world charm it exuded.

'Now, let me see,' mused Suzanne thoughtfully as she slid back a wardrobe door to reveal a rack filled with so many gowns that it defied description as far as her companion was concerned. 'Green would be best, I think, but not too dark so that it competes with those eyes of yours. Ah-hah, I know, I've got just the thing!' she exclaimed triumphantly, and began sorting through them rapidly in her bid to locate the one she wanted before withdrawing a particular creation and asking, 'How does that appeal?'

'It's beautiful, absolutely beautiful,' Paige sighed eloquently, but no matter how hard she tried couldn't stop herself from wondering how much it had cost. One thing was for certain, it hadn't come off a peg from even the most expensive of stores!

'It should fit, seeing we look about the same size, but maybe you'd better try it on, just in case,' Suzanne continued. 'In the meantime, I'll pick out an assortment of other clothes you're likely to need while you're here.'

Paige hunched her shoulders deprecatingly. 'I seem to be putting you to a tremendous amount of trouble.'

'It's the least we can do since you lost all your own gear on one of our properties,' Suzanne smiled, and headed for the other end of the wardrobe where she began extracting hangers adorned with slacks and shirts.

'Not through any fault of yours, though,' Paige protested as she slipped out of the bathrobe and into the dress. 'If I'd taken your brother's advice in the first place none of this would be happening.'

'Oh, well, that's the way it goes. Sometimes we listen, and sometimes we don't,' Suzanne waved aside her acceptance of blame offhandedly. 'How does the dress look?'

Paige didn't immediately answer, she was still surveying her image appraisingly in the full-length mirror beside the dressing table. The dress fitted as if made for her, the wide neckline plunging to a form-fitting band beneath her breasts, the skirt flaring around her ankles in a froth of multi-layered chiffon. And the colour couldn't have been better. Rich peppermint green covered by a diaphanous white overlay, it complemented but didn't subdue the brilliance of her wide-spaced eyes as they stared back at her in silent wonderment. How on earth could one relatively simply designed gown create such an illusion of breathtaking femininity?

'You like?' prompted Suzanne.

'I like!' she nodded emphatically.

With her head angled consideringly the older girl concluded her scrutiny. 'Actually, I think it looks better on you than it does on me. You've got slightly more cleavage.'

'You don't think it's a little—er—too revealing?' Paige swallowed selfconsciously.

'Good heavens! Whatever are you suggesting?' Suzanne threw up her hands in feigned shock. 'Madame Véranique would never allow one of her unparalleled

masterpieces to be so indecorous as to show *too* much!
No, it's perfect just as it is, and with the right amount
of make-up—we'll borrow some of Michelle's, mine
would be too dark for you—you'll knock their eyes out.'

'I'm not sure I want to,' wryly. 'This evening, especially, I think I would rather be as unobtrusive as possible.'

'But that's just the point,' Suzanne wagged a finger
at her significantly. 'Whether you want it or not, you're
going to be the centre of attention tonight, so you may
as well do it in style.'

'Because of my slapping Kelly?'

'Yes, well, I can't say that won't have whetted their
interest, but mainly because you're that wonder of
wonders, a new face! Three days of isolation and this
crowd has been at each other's throats ever since. I
only wish they'd left with the intelligent ones, while
the planes could still take off, but they didn't, and
now they're ravenous for . . .'

'Someone else to tear to pieces?'

'Well, probably not on your first night,' Suzanne
quipped banteringly. 'Although I'd still tread warily
where Nadine is concerned, if I were you. She hasn't
been exactly happy knowing Kelly was stranded with
an extremely attractive redhead, nor with the fact that
he apparently wasn't in any great hurry to return
either, what's more.'

'But that was only because he wanted to be certain
we'd make it in one day,' Paige demurred. 'Besides,
why should she care? They're divorced, aren't they?'

'At his instigation, though, not hers. I rather think
she wouldn't be averse to trying her luck a second time
around.'

'Oh, I see.' Paige moved restlessly, her eyes losing some of their lustre. And if Nadine was willing to make the effort who could say what Kelly's reaction might be? He must have been in love with her at one time.

'Mmm, now you know the reason for my warning. It could have been embarrassing for you if you'd inadvertently found yourself becoming the ham in the sandwich just because Nadine had decided you might be a threat to her plans.'

Paige's laughter was unusually brittle. 'Apart from the fact that I never was a threat, she couldn't possibly believe he'd want anything more to do with me after *my* effort this afternoon. I doubt he'll even speak to me again!'

'Would you want him to?'

The unexpectedly shrewd query had her catching her breath as all the pain and confusion his behaviour had caused surged to the fore again. 'Not particularly— except to say goodbye!' she retorted throatily after only a moment's hesitation.

'Then I'm probably warning you for nothing,' Suzanne smiled, pulling open a dresser drawer and adding still more clothes to the ever mounting pile. 'There, I think that should keep you going for a while, but if there's anything else you need don't, for heaven's sake, be backward in letting me know, will you?'

Paige scooped up a mound and began moving towards the door. 'I can't imagine what else there is to need,' she half smiled. She now had more than she'd originally brought with her in the car. 'You've been more than generous.'

Suzanne led the way back across the hall and laid her

bundle on the bed before glancing up with an enigmatic expression. 'But not in a patronising fashion, I hope. Kelly said I should play it very low key.'

'Oh?' Paige halted, frowning. 'When did he say that?'

'Last night when he called in.'

'Did he also happen to say why?'

'Mmm, and that's the funny part,' Suzanne began pensively. 'He said—more or less—that you were so independant you'd probably be upset if you thought I was being too charitable and he didn't want that to happen.' Her lips pursed wryly and she sent Paige a quizzical look. 'Now wasn't that a strange thing for him to have cared about if he's been amusing himself at your expense all this time?'

CHAPTER SEVEN

WHEN Suzanne returned with the promised make-up they both avoided any reference to her previous parting remark as if by common consent—Paige, because her thoughts and emotions were now too turbulent to make any comment at all, and Suzanne, she suspected, from a desire not to intrude. On their way to the sitting room for a drink before dinner there wasn't time to dwell on the thought-provoking subject either, because Paige needed all her concentration to steel herself against the coming meeting with her host. No matter what Kelly might have intimated the evening before—or his reason for doing so—she had no doubt he wouldn't be so considerate tonight!

The sound of sudden laughter above the muted murmur of conversation just as they arrived at the doorway, followed by a sharp discordant riposte, had Suzanne's brows peaking expressively.

'They're at it again,' she grinned.

'Why don't you fly them out in the helicopter?' Paige queried. 'Kelly said you had one.'

'True,' Suzanne nodded. 'But wouldn't you know it? It's out on loan to a friend of ours over in S.A. at the moment and it's not expected back for another couple of weeks. By then the ground should be okay for the other aircraft to take off without any trouble,' she advised ruefully. 'Besides, it should improve now that Kelly's back, because it was really only due to Nadine's persuading that he allowed them to stay here in the first place when we thought the Races would still be able to be held. But he was fighting mad, believe me, when he discovered they'd elected to remain behind when the others left. They'll want to watch themselves from here on or there'll be a few feathers flying before very much longer. My brother isn't exactly reticent when he's been pushed beyond the limit!'

A reminder she could well have done without right at present, Paige decided glumly, and sought to dismiss it from her mind as quickly as possible by asking, 'But why *was* Kelly at the outstation? It's a little odd for the owner of such a large holding to be working as a stockman, or whatever, isn't it?'

'Not really,' she was informed with a smile. 'The larger they are the more manpower they need, and

Kelly's the type who likes to get out there and make things happen, not wait for them to come to him. So when it became necessary to send someone over to Bindaburra he decided to go himself—not only because he wanted a full and accurate report on the state of the whole property, but also because I suspect he likes to get away from Ainslie and it's restrictions every once in a while in order to return to the basics, so to speak.'

Suddenly an arm was thrown around each of their waists as one of Nadine's friends edged between them from behind.

'Come on in, ladies, we can't have two of the best-looking females here depriving us of their presence for the sake of a mere conversation!' he exclaimed in exuberant bonhomie as he urged them forwards. 'What would you like to drink, hmm?'

Realising they had no choice but to join the rest of the guests both girls smiled their acquiescence and named their preferences, Paige's breathing quickening when she saw the direction in which Suzanne intended leading them while they waited for their self-appointed steward to return. Kelly and his mother were standing slightly to one side of the nearest group containing Nadine and another couple, both of them looking extremely polished in evening dress and both appearing unconsciously self-assured—the very thing Paige was not.

She greeted them with a smile which was supposed to be carefree, but which she surmised was dismally crooked, then suffered Kelly's cold assessment with a defiantly proud lift of her head as the grey of his eyes visibly phased out the blue as his dissecting gaze swept over her. She figured she had just as much right

to be infuriated over what had happened—if not more!
—as he had.

'That dress suits you very well, Paige,' Michelle's soft
voice finally captured her attention. 'It's fortunate Suzanne is able to lend you some of her clothes.'

'Yes, and I'm very grateful,' she smiled, more posi-
tively this time.

'But don't you find it embarrassing having to rely
on someone else for cast-offs? I know I would,' cooed
Nadine, her arrival heralded by a rustling of blue
silk as she linked arms with her ex-husband.

'Hardly a cast-off, Nadine,' Suzanne was quick to
correct. 'It's never been worn before.'

'Even if it was, it's certainly better than the sheets I
had to use when I was at Bindaburra,' Paige came in
a close second, then sent the man facing her a goading
glance. 'And which I will replace as soon as I'm able
to.'

Kelly's expression darkened ominously. 'You try, and
I'll . . .'

'Here you go!' A genial voice interrupted fortuit-
ously, and Paige abruptly found a cocktail-filled glass
being thrust into her hand, as was Suzanne, by their
obliging waiter as he caught up with them. 'You get
yourselves around those and I guarantee they'll put an
edge on your appetite for another of Ainslie's delec-
table repasts tonight.'

'Oh, God, don't you ever think of anything but your
stomach, Vaughan?' Nadine drawled in bored dispar-
agement, her eyes turning skywards.

'No, can't say I do, lovey,' the rather portly middle-
aged man replied unconcernedly. 'But it sure beats the
hell out of sitting around all day sharpening claws just

so you can sink them into somebody when they're least
prepared.' Without giving anyone a chance to speak
he then turned to Paige to extol, 'Now this little darling—no pun intended, sweetheart—I'm willing to bet
has a nature as sweet as her name . . .'

'Apart from when she's slapping other women's hus-
bands, of course!' Nadine couldn't resist inserting.

'Ex!' amended Suzanne, giving Paige cause to look
at her speculatively. So that was who had said it earlier.

'Ah, yes, but I'm sure she had good reason,' Vaughan
continued excusingly, and glancing up at Kelly's far
greater height shook his head in mock distaste. 'These
tall husky men are always the very devil, aren't they,
sweetheart?' he asked of Paige.

She nodded weakly, starting to laugh at his exagger-
ated grimace—as was everyone else except for Nadine
—and offered no resistance when he suggestd, 'Then
allow me to escort you to a seat over there,' indicating
a chocolate velvet upholstered sofa, 'thus enabling our
twin souls to amiability to communicate without inter-
ruption from those with less agreeable thoughts on
their minds.'

With a politely murmured, 'Excuse me,' Paige
allowed herself to be led away. Vaughan's company
promised to be somewhat more relaxing than Nadine
and Kelly's!

'There now, isn't that better than being shredded by
our little blonde she-wolf?' he joked after seeing her
seated.

A look back at the group they had just left collided
with that of one very grim-faced male and she swiftly
redirected her gaze. 'Much,' she smiled gratefully. 'But

if you think of her in those terms why did you come here with her?'

His mouth twisted puckishly. 'Would you believe, because I'm in love with her?'

On the verge of answering with a decided negative, she stopped and looked at him closely. 'Are you?' she frowned.

'Just as much as you are with that handsome brute standing next to her.'

His return was made so conversationally that Paige could hardly credit what she was hearing, and almost choked on the mouthful of drink she had been taking.

'G-good grief! Whatever gave you that idea?' she gasped unsteadily.

'Observation, and that peculiar insight one—shall we say, unrequited?—lover has for another,' he relayed whimsically. 'But don't worry, your secret's safe with me. I told you we had twin souls, didn't I?'

And she'd thought his company was going to be *relaxing*! Paige cleared the tight lump of dismay from her throat and admitted nothing, preferring to ask instead, 'Have you told her how you feel?'

'There's no need,' he shrugged. 'She already knows.'

'Oh, I'm sorry,' she commiserated earnestly—partly because she knew what he was going through, and partly because of the callous way Nadine had treated him.

'Not yet you shouldn't be,' he suddenly smiled again, his natural ebullience reasserting itself. 'If you can take that ex-husband of hers out of the running for me, then I figure I've got a better than even chance of making her see things my way.'

'But, Vaughan, you can't pin your hopes on me!' she protested, aghast. 'I mean absolutely nothing to Kelly. In fact, he doesn't even *like* me!'

'Not at all?' he probed disbelievingly, and not a little disappointed..

'Does it look like it?' she countered wryly, seeing the subject of their discussion turning towards them again.

'Oh, well, I'll just have to make the best of it and continue as before, I guess,' he sighed, but without seeming too upset at the prospect, much to Paige's astonishment. 'You never know, she just might come round to my way of thinking in time.'

'I hope so . . . if that's what you want.'

He chuckled in recognition of her slight hesitancy and levered himself to his feet. 'Meanwhile, I shall partake of a glass of wine and savour my food with a gourmet's appreciation, as usual.' Bending forward, he extended a hand towards her. 'If you would care to take my arm, Miss Darling, it will be my pleasure to escort you into the dining room. I believe dinner is about to be served.'

'Why, thank you, Mr . . .' She halted and looked at him apologetically. 'I'm very sorry, but I'm afraid I can't remember your surname. There were so many introductions this afternoon.'

'It's Murchison,' he supplied with a slight movement of his head. 'Vaughan Murchison.'

'Then thank you, Mr Murchison.' She linked her arm with his with a smile. 'I shall be honoured to accompany you in to dinner.'

As they followed their hosts into the graciously ornate dining room Paige looked about her wonderingly, and a trifle sardonically. It was a far cry from where she had had dinner the previous evening, and as she took her seat at the long, polished, and precisely laid rosewood table she tried ruefully to identify the man at the head of the table—ruler of a family empire and waited on by his own staff—with the person she had known as a stockman and cook on a lonely outstation.

'Do tell us what it was like while you were incarcerated at Bindaburra, we're all anxiously waiting to hear. Was it terribly boring?' A brunette on the opposite side of the table brought Paige out of her reverie as soon as their entrées had been served.

'Yes, what *did* you find to do all day?' prompted someone else from further along.

Paige shrugged, wondering what they expected her to have done all day. 'I tidied and cleaned the house, made myself some things to wear, went for walks, helped do some painting, all kinds of things. But no, I didn't find it at all boring,' she declared firmly.

'It sounds it,' a girl tittered.

'I expect that's because you're not accustomed to having to perform such humble tasks, Andrea. Each to his or her own, you know,' Nadine smiled condescendingly from her position beside Kelly. 'Paige is probably happiest when she's scrubbing floors and washing dishes.'

'No,' Paige began, and struck a pose of thoughtful reflection. 'I would say I'm probably happiest when I'm enjoying a good meal and pleasant conversation in congenial company,' she gibed sweetly.

A few covert grins appeared as Nadine's supercilious smirk changed to narrow-eyed rancour, but it was all completely lost on the brunette with the somewhat vacuous features across the table as she queried disappointedly, 'But surely that can't be all that happened while you were there. Wasn't there any excitement at all?'

'Well, I guess that depends on whether you call being treed by an enraged bull exciting, or frightening,' Paige replied drily.

'You weren't!'

'I don't think I'd care for that much!'

'You mean, it actually chased you?'

'Goodness, whatever did you do?'

'*I* didn't do much at all, actually,' she revealed when the rapid burst of comments finally ceased. 'Kelly shot it.'

'With a gun?' It was the brunette again.

'Don't be such a fool, Emma! Of course with a gun! You'd hardly expect him to use a bow and arrow, would you?' jeered Nadine, apparently willing to vent her peevishness on anyone at the moment.

'I only asked,' the girl called Emma hunched one shoulder deprecatingly. 'If you don't ask, you don't learn.'

The look which followed said all to plainly that Nadine doubted she would anyway, and then Michelle was interposing solicitously.

'I hope you weren't hurt at all, Paige.'

'Only my dignity at having to turn and run,' she half laughed. 'Although it's not an experience I'd care to repeat. It was quite frightening at the time.'

'I can imagine,' Michelle smiled understandingly, and sent her son an almost accusing look. 'You didn't tell us about this, Kelly,' she frowned.

The subtle flexing of his shoulders was sardonic, the

wide sweep of his mouth disparaging in Paige's eyes. 'Knowing how fast the news would have travelled, I wouldn't have liked Stuart to worry and think I wasn't looking after his—er—guest with the proper amount of care,' he drawled.

Liar! Paige's eyes sparkled angrily down the length of the table. That was just one of her own gibes he was repaying her with! The only thing that had ever concerned him while they'd been at Bindaburra was that she shouldn't be given the chance to exploit what he mistakenly believed to be her mercenary reasons for journeying all this way!

Apparently Michelle found his reply quite reasonable, though, because she accepted it unquestioningly, and went on to say. 'That reminds me, did you remember to tell Paige that Stuart was asking after her this evening?' And to Paige herself, 'Kelly said you would probably have a word with him some time tomorrow. He thought you would rather rest before dinner this evening since you'd had such a long trip today.'

'Oh, that *was* thoughtful of him,' Paige smiled as best she could through gritted teeth, her ire mounting at yet another instance of his interfering arbitrariness. 'But at what time tomorrow do you think you'll be in touch with Greenvale? If I know in advance I can make certain I'm available to speak to him.'

'It could be any time. I'll let you know,' Kelly advised negligently.

'Please do,' she warbled dulcetly, but not without a thread of tartness in her tone. 'I wouldn't like to miss him again.'

His slow answering smile, totally unexpected and

provokingly enticing, had her heart pumping blood agonisingly through her veins as anger fought a losing battle against attraction. Kelly had no intention of letting her know, and not only did they both know it, but more annoyingly, they were also both aware that there was very little she could do about it without creating a scene, or appearing to be trying to cause trouble! He had only to say he hadn't been able to locate her at the time and there was no way she could prove he deliberately hadn't bothered to look. Resentfully, she returned her attention to her meal.

As course followed unhurriedly upon course it became obvious that the other guests' interest in Paige's experiences was waning until Suzanne, of all people, innocently fanned it into blazing life again.

'So what did you do with the bed, take it in turns?' she enquired laughingly. 'I know only one was sent out.'

Paige stared back at her numbly, unable to formulate a response because the constricting muscles of her throat seemed to be strangling her, and praying her face wasn't as red as it felt. In desperation she cast pleading eyes towards the head of the table. Surely he couldn't be so unfeeling as to leave her to satisfy their avid curiosity alone!

For a moment, as their glances locked, it appeared he was going to do just that and her eyelids flickered down desolately, only to flash upwards again a mere second later in gratitude and relief when she realised Kelly had begun to speak.

'No, as there was only a limited amount of bedding available we took the most sensible approach and shared,' he answered curtly, his expression informing his sister all too explicitly what he thought of her unthinking question.

'That must have been cosy,' a man's voice insinuated slyly, rashly, in the light of Kelly's squashing tones.

'Extremely!' snapped Nadine, uncaring, and looked daggers at Paige.

'Then you obviously have very little perception!' Kelly slated contemptuously, his mouth levelling to a threatening line. 'It was neither cosy nor particularly comfortable... it was simply expedient! And if any-one has ideas to the contrary, I don't suggest they give tongue to them in my hearing!' A challenging scrutiny of arctic frigidity encompassed everyone present.

Even Nadine didn't quite dare ignore that biting caution, no matter how much she might have liked to, and to Paige's heartfelt thankfulness the meal was finally concluded in comparative peace and without her again becoming the centre of attention.

Suzanne, however, could hardly wait until they had adjourned to the sitting room for coffee before joining Paige on a couch beside the open french doors.

'God, I am sorry for putting you in such an embar-rassing position,' she apologised immediately. 'I would have realised you'd share the damned bed if I'd only stopped and thought about it first. It was the obvious thing to do under the circumstances.'

'Oh, well, there's no harm done,' Paige shrugged, and smiled. 'I think Kelly managed to convince most of them that their original thoughts were somewhat wide of the mark?

'Amen to that!' Suzanne seconded with expressive

fervency. 'As it is, I reckon I can expect a few brief but forthright remarks from my dear brother for bringing up the subject at all.'

'But you weren't to know.'

'Whether I did or not doesn't really matter. Having recalled only one bed being taken over, I should also have remembered the number of blankets and such which accompanied it, and kept my mouth shut instead of happily envisaging him being turned out of his bed by an unexpected visitor!'

'No such luck,' grimaced Paige drily. 'He didn't even make the offer.'

'No? Well, I suppose there wasn't much point, all things considered.' Suzanne stirred her coffee thoughtfully and then sent her an engaging grin. 'What did you think of Vaughan? He's a strange little man, isn't he?'

Paige nodded and smiled. 'But kinder than most of the others, I think.'

'Oh, yes, he and Emma—the one who was asking all the inane questions—are the pick of the bunch. She's a little bit on the dumb side, but at least she isn't spiteful. As for Vaughan,' she gave her head a confused shake, 'well, I can't quite make up my mind about him. I suppose he told you he's in love with Nadine?' And when Paige had affirmed the supposition, 'I thought he probably would have, he hadn't been here for more than five minutes before he was telling me all about it and asking me to put in a good word for him with her.' Paige could have mentioned that he'd asked her to go one better than that, but as his suggestion ran too closely parallel with her own desires she decided against saying anything about it. 'Anyway, after seeing the way she's treated him for this last couple of weeks I can't decide whether he's a hero or a fool. How he puts up with what she hands out I really don't know.'

With her eyes surreptitiously following Kelly's commanding figure on the other side of the room Paige answered without thinking.

'Maybe he just can't control who he falls in love with... like a great many of the rest of us,' she surmised cheerlessly.

Suzanne peered at her shrewdly. 'Do I detect a wistful note of personal disillusionment in that remark?' she probed.

'Good lord, no!' Realising how she must have sounded, Paige rapidly discounted the idea with a forced laugh. 'I was expounding a theory, that's all. And perhaps feeling a little sorry for Vaughan. He seems such an inoffensive person,' she added for camouflage.

'Mmm, although he can put her in her place sometimes when he feels like it, as you saw earlier,' Suzanne pointed out 'Who knows? If he did it a little more often, she might even be forced into respecting him for it.'

'Has she always been so...' about to say 'bitchy', Paige modified it to, 'catty?'

'No, not always, although she's never liked being refused her own way, of course. She and Kelly used to have some tremendous rows when he wouldn't let her do exactly as she pleased, without caring whether it suited or inconvenienced anyone else or not.'

There was one question which had been hovering on Paige's lips for some time, and now she just had to ask it. 'Do you think there's a likelihood of them marrying again?'

'I shouldn't think so,' Suzanne frowned thoughtfully, pondering the matter. 'Quite frankly, I was surprised when he married her the first time. I may be wrong, of course, but I've often thought he only did it because he was sorry for her.'

'Oh?' It wasn't possible for Paige to disguise her interest.

'Yes, her father had just died from a heart attack after discovering he'd poured every last cent they owned into some bogus mining venture, and since her mother and Michelle had been friends for many years what better shoulder to cry out your woes on than that of my good-natured brother. Who not only happened to be single, but conveniently—or should I have said, essentially?—had the wherewithal necessary to make life bearable again for poor tragic little Miss Cardwell.' Suzanne gibed sarcastically.

'You really think she only married him for his money?' Was that why he distrusted *her* motives for visiting Stuart so strongly? Because he himself had been snared in just such a trap?

'Well, perhaps not entirely. After all, sister or not, I do realise he has other attributes which aren't exactly repellent to the opposite sex,' Suzanne granted drily. 'But in general terms, yes, that is my opinion. Of course, whether Kelly thinks or knows any different is something else again. On personal matters he's remarkably like a clam!' She shrugged impassively. 'For all I know, I may be doing her a great injustice by even suggesting such a thing, but somehow my feminine instincts tell me I'm not.'

'Yet he's still willing to give her and her friends the free run of your home,' Paige put forward tentatively.

Suzanne's roguish smile set her deep brown eyes twinkling. 'I prefer to think of him as being *unwilling* to deny her the use of it during social events,' she laughed. 'For the one or two visits she makes each year I figure he reckons he can afford to be obliging.' Her expression suddenly sobered. 'Don't look now, but I believe we're about to become the recipients of the dubious honour of my loving ex-sister-in-law's invigorating presence. I can see her heading this way.'

'That's nice,' was all Paige had time to mock before the blue-eyed blonde was upon them, a cup of coffee precariously balanced in her hand.

'My, but you two are having quite a tête-à-tête over here, aren't you?' she smiled down at them with false friendliness. 'Whatever can it be that's so private the rest of us aren't allowed to hear? More of Paige's less publishable experiences with my husband, perhaps?' considerably less friendly.

'*Ex*-husband!'

Nadine momentarily closed her eyes in a gesture of long-suffering. 'You know, Suzanne, I'm finding that childish amendment of yours becoming quite tedious,' she sighed. 'So why don't you keep your nose out of matters which don't concern you and give it a rest for a while?'

'Oh, I will, Nadine, I will,' Suzanne acceded effusively, but in a goading tone. 'As soon as you stop laying claim to a relationship which no longer exists!'

'I notice Kelly doesn't complain,' the blonde remarked smugly.

'No? Well, maybe he's better at hiding his feelings

than I am,' Suzanne quipped facetiously. 'I still shouldn't take too much for granted, though, if I were you. You did that once before, remember? and finished up with egg all over your face!'

The blue eyes narrowed to glittering slits and it was obviously only with difficulty that Nadine retained her complacent pose. 'Oh, I wouldn't say that,' she crowed eventually. 'It suited me to regain my freedom at the time, and money-wise it was certainly worth my while, you must admit. Not like it's been for some I could mention.' Her gaze slid pointedly, jeeringly, to the other occupant of the couch.

'Meaning?' Paige asked tautly.

'Oh, don't be coy, sweetie,' Nadine laughed archly, and took a sip of her coffee. 'Everyone could read between the lines of what Kelly had to say during dinner, and we realise how disappointed and utterly humiliated you must be. All those services rendered and not a thing to show for it except a loaned dress ... and even that donation had to come from his *sister*!' Another tinkling laugh and she gibed, 'Not quite the. repayment you'd anticipated, I'm sure.'

'You're so right!' Paige eyed her with distaste, both for the person and the implication. 'But as your obviously polluted mentality can't differentiate between two people sharing a bed for the sake of expedience, and two people sleeping together for the sake of dalliance, then *I'm* sure it would be a complete waste of my time trying to explain to you just what I did expect!' she retorted scornfully.

'So it's a polluted mentality I've got for not being taken in by that trumped-up story, is it?' Nadine's voice sharpened sarcastically, her annoyance in no wise lessened by Suzanne's stifled laughter. 'Well, let me tell you something, you brazen little tramp! You're nothing but an unwanted interloper from the ranks of the peasantry, dressed up in borrowed finery just so you could be permitted to sit at the same table as your betters!'

Uncaring of the interested looks they were drawing, Paige's retaliation was delivered with biting sarcasm. 'I'd rather be that than an alimony-grabbing leech who openly boasts of her mercenary prowess!'

'What did you say?'

If she hadn't heard Paige's reply then everyone in the room certainly heard Nadine's enraged question, and saw her violent reprisal as she bent to send a forceful hand swinging towards Paige's head—a blow which connected sharply with her cheek, the action toppling Nadine's cup of coffee into her lap.

'Get out of here, Nadine, before I'm tempted to do the same to you!' hissed Suzanne furiously amid the general commotion as she disposed of the cup and saucer on a nearby table so Paige could rise to her feet.

Nadine immediately put her hands over her face and began sobbing copious tears, but still managing to see Kelly, who was the first to reach them, and to propel herself brokenheartedly into his arms as if she had been the one attacked.

With one side of her face feeling on fire Paige wiped hot coffee from her arm with her fingers and looked down at the dark stain marking the dress she was wearing in dismay.

'Oh, Suzanne, I'm so sorry,' she murmured contritely. 'Your beautiful dress is ruined!'

'Never mind, if it is I'll charge it to Nadine,' the other girl threatened, glaring at the blue-clad figure still clinging to her brother as he and Vaughan led her away through the gathering guests.

''More importantly, how are you, Paige?' questioned Michelle on overhearing their conversation as she joined them. 'Did that coffee burn?'

'No, luckily it was only hot, not boiling,' she half smiled. Her arm wasn't burning anywhere near as much as her face was! 'I'll be okay, it's Suzanne's dress I'm worried about. Do you think it will be possible to remove the stain?'

'We can always give it a try,' she was advised encouragingly as the three of them began heading for the doorway. 'Suzanne can take it down to the laundry while you change.' A few minutes later, on reaching the hall, she apologised soberly, 'I really am very sorry for what happened, Paige. I can't think what came over Nadine to act in such a manner.'

About to confess that the other girl might have had reason, Paige noticed Suzanne giving a warning shake of her head in the background, and desisted. But when the two of them were presently making for her room she couldn't help returning to the matter.

'Why didn't you want me to say anything?' she asked. 'I mean, Nadine *was* provoked, wasn't she? Maybe she saw it in the light of an eye for an eye since I'd done the same to Kelly this afternoon,' wryly.

'Hah! As if Nadine's thoughts were ever occupied by anyone but herself! Besides, why should we give her an out? If she can't take the consequences she shouldn't go looking for trouble. She wasn't exactly complimentary or appeasing herself, if you recall!'

'Mmm, I somehow gained the impression she doesn't think much of me,' Paige suddenly laughed, opening the door and entering her room.

'Well, don't let it worry you,' Suzanne advocated, checking in the mirror to tuck a few tendrils of hair back into place while Paige divested herself of the dress. 'I doubt there's many people Nadine harbours kind thoughts for, and especially among her own sex.'

Dressed in the bathrobe, Paige held out Suzanne's soiled gown apologetically. 'Once again, I am sorry, but—but would you mind very much if I called it a day? It has been somewhat eventful, and I'm rather tired after that journey.'

'No, of course I don't mind. All things considered, I'm surprised you didn't pack it in straight after dinner,' Suzanne smiled understandingly as she prepared to leave. 'We'll see you in the morning. Sleep well.' With the door almost closed behind her, she stopped and put her head back inside. 'Do you ride, by the way?'

'No, no, I don't,' Paige shook her head ruefully.

'Oh, that's a pity. Kelly and I usually go riding first thing every morning when he's at home and I thought you might like to join us.'

'It's very nice of you to offer, but ...' Paige spread her hands wide in assumed regret. Even if she had been able to ride she would have been making an excuse to avoid Kelly's company. Perhaps the less she saw of him the less she would think about him, and the sooner she would be able to pick up the threads of her old life again.

'Well, maybe I could give you lessons,' Suzanne now suggested helpfully. 'At least it's one way for you to fill in some time during the days ahead.'

'I guess it would do that,' mused Paige speculatively. 'Although I don't know that I'd be any good at it. On both occasions when I've doubled up with Kelly I've—er—found myself wholeheartedly wishing I was somewhere else.'

'But was that because of the horse, or my brother?' joked Suzanne.

It wasn't something Paige could treat humorously, however, and she was only able to dredge up a pensive half smile in response. 'Perhaps a combination of both,' she owned unsteadily.

Suzanne's gaze narrowed with a frown, but she didn't press the point. 'Well, you have a think about it and let me know. There's no rush to decide right at the moment.'

Paige made ready for bed slowly, her mind as chaotic as her feelings. Her initial burst of anger at Kelly's deception had dissipated long ago and now only the hurt remained behind to turn her insides into an emotional battleground where logic and rationalisation were running a poor second to the overpowering ache of unfulfilled longing.

It didn't matter how hard she tried to prevent it she couldn't keep his tormenting image from flooding her mind. He filled her thoughts entirely, and when she answered a knock on her door—expecting it to be Suzanne again—but found herself face to face with the actuality and not the image she could only stare up at him in wide-eyed helplessness, her brain a totally unco-operative blank.

'I came to check how you were.' Kelly was the first to speak, his eyes assessing as they ranged over her stiffly held figure, his tone perfunctory. 'Suzanne said you wouldn't be joining us again tonight.'

'Th-that's right,' she managed to confirm, but only after two hasty swallows. 'I thought I would have an early night. It's been a long day.'

'You're okay?'

Was that a note of concern she could detect? Paige shrugged inwardly and dismissed the idea as wishful thinking. 'Yes, I'm fine ... thank you,' she whispered miserably, wishing he would leave and yet, at the same time, contrarily hoping that he wouldn't.

Her chin was suddenly tipped upwards by a lean hard hand. 'Are you sure? You don't look to be in particularly fine fettle to me.'

She didn't feel it either! 'I've just removed my make-up, so perhaps that has something to do with it,' she parried.

'Oh, don't give me that!' His voice roughened with impatience. 'I *know* what you look like without make-up, remember? and it isn't like a pale ghost!' When she didn't reply he sighed audibly and released her chin in order to smooth the tips of his fingers gently, disturbingly, across her creamy-skinned cheek. 'I'm sorry Nadine lashed out at you. I ...'

'It doesn't matter,' she cut in swiftly, putting more distance between them before she forgot his gesture didn't mean anything to him—hadn't she learnt anything from past experience?—and remembering all too despondently that it had been his ex-wife who received all his consideration after the incident. 'The only damage done was to Suzanne's dress. I'm quite all right, *really*! Just a little tired, that's all.'

'And you would rather I left?'

Against all her inclinations she clipped out her response almost as coldly as he had his question. 'Yes.'

But when she had the room all to herself again her fragile control finally broke, and it was with hot despairing tears overflowing her lashes that she curled beneath the bedclothes and tried to make believe she didn't miss the exciting feel of his long muscular body beside her, nor the possessive but strangely reassuring arm thrown across her midriff.

CHAPTER EIGHT

AFTER four days of holding her head high and giving the impression she either didn't notice, or didn't care, that she and Kelly were hardly on speaking terms, Paige began making excuses to stay in her room—or at least the homestead—whenever possible. Not only was Kelly's coolness beginning to tear her in two, but watching Nadine attempting to ingratiate herself with him—and with his apparent approval—was something she just couldn't bear to watch any more.

So, when Suzanne enquired one lunchtime if she wanted to join those who were willing to summon up the energy to walk down to the yards to see another brumby the stockmen had brought in being educated to the saddle, she declined and said she had a headache because she knew without a doubt that both Kelly and Nadine would be among those present.

'Can I get you something for it?' Suzanne asked sympathetically as they left the dining room together.

'No, I'll be okay, thanks all the same,' Paige evaded uncomfortably at having to pretend. 'A rest in a darkened room usually clears them without too much trouble.'

'You often have them, do you?'

'Er...' As quite the opposite was the case Paige had to cast about frantically for inspiration and eventually came up with her mother's often quoted, 'Only when I've been out in the sun for too long.'

'Oh, you should have said something. We needn't have stayed down at the tennis courts so long this morning.'

'But I enjoyed our games, and—and it doesn't always give them to me.'

Thankful when they at last reached her room, Paige bade the other girl a hasty and guilty farewell and slipped inside as hurriedly as she could. She disliked intensely having to prevaricate, and especially since Suzanne had been so open and kind towards her, but it just wasn't possible for her to continue feigning an indifference to Kelly she didn't feel.

For an hour or more she stayed in her room, either futilely attempting to read or pacing aimlessly around the floor, but the lure of the sun-bright vista visible beyond the french doors was irresistible. Stepping cautiously out on to the verandah, she peered along its length for any signs of life, and then across the gardens to the line of tall trees which acted as a windbreak for the homestead against the westerly winds which could sweep so ferociously over the landscape. Today they weren't needed, however, and their leaves hung still and dusty in the hot dry air, but the shade beneath them looked cool and inviting, so, with one last swift encompassing glance, she half hurried and half crept from the verandah to the path which led towards them.

When the path headed towards a steel gate which opened into a paddock beside the trees Paige veered to her right, following the fence until the homestead was lost from view. A little further along she stepped over a bore drain where the water flowed smoothly and into a small clearing. On the other side of the fence a horse was making good use of the man-made stream and she stared at it intently.

'Mercury?' she part called, part pondered, moving closer to the wooden rails which separated them.

The big black gelding raised his proud head and eyed her askance, almost as if deliberating whether he would condescend to fully acknowledge her presence or not. Then, after having apparently decided that he had nothing better to do, he began ambling haughtily towards her.

'Oh, Mercury, it is you,' she murmured as she stretched out a hand to pat his arched neck, tears springing to her eyes. Goodness knows why, you must be insane, she chided herself wryly. It wasn't even as if she had enjoyed the time she had spent on his back.

Nonetheless, he was a link to the time when she had been on far better terms with his master and for that reason she was reluctant to move on. How long she stayed there stroking his shiny hide and talking inconsequentially to him she had no idea, but he seemed to accept—or was it suffer?—her attentions willingly enough, so she remained.

The unmistakable sound of creaking saddle leather

and the clip of hooves eventually advised of someone's approach, but she didn't lift her head, hoping that if it was one of the stockmen they would ride on without disturbing her, and thus allow her the chance to wipe away the unbidden tears which still spiked her lashes before having to face anyone.

'I thought you were supposed to have a headache.'

There was no need for her to turn around to discover the identity of the speaker. Only one person had a drawl that could unbalance her so easily, and this time was no different from the others as her breathing raced erratically.

'I—I have,' she whispered throatily, and feeling it wasn't a lie because the throbbing at her temples was certainly no lighter than the pounding of her heart at the moment.

'Caused by too much sun, so I'm told.'

The irony in his tone increased, as did the strength of his voice, and combined with the rest of the sounds she could hear Paige knew he had urged his mount considerably closer.

'Yes,' she tried to inject a little more positiveness into her reply even as she dashed the tips of her fingers quickly across her wet lashes.

'And the best remedy for that, of course, is to stand in the blazing heat in the hottest part of the day, is it?'

A gentle nudge at her shoulder and a soft snort in her ear informed Paige just how much nearer they were this time and she inched further along the rails, still without taking her eyes from the horse she continued to pat abstractedly.

'I was feeling a little better, so I decided to go for

a walk,' she shrugged in what she hoped was a dismissive manner.

'In the sun, without a hat?' Kelly charged, sarcasm the overriding force now.

'I can if I want to,' she flared, chancing a hasty look and finding to her agitation that he was dismounting. 'It's my prerogative, isn't it?'

'The same as it was your prerogative to slap my face for having misled *you*?'

Unsure as to his intention, Paige relinquished all pretence of interest in Mercury in order to keep a wary eye on Kelly's approach. Since she had just drawn a disturbing comparison between his deception and her own, now was definitely not the time to turn her back on him!

'I d-don't know what you mean,' she denied, albeit not very convincingly.

'No?' A lazy smile played about his lips which had her staring at him in a mixture of fascination and trepidation. Why was he suddenly volunteering to speak to her now, after all these days of silence?

'No!' she almost shouted in return, regaining control of her senses at last and starting to back away. 'All right, so I shouldn't have hit you, I—I'm sorry, but you— but you ...' She halted with a nervous cry as she saw his hand streaking out towards her and, spinning about, she raced for what she hoped was the refuge of the trees.

It was a forlorn expectation and before she could even make it past the dappled shade created by the outer branches of a drooping desert oak she had been pulled down amid the newly sprouting grass, her hair spilling around her like a russet cloud. Within seconds her furious struggles had been quelled. One arm was securely pinned beneath Kelly's powerful frame, the other held in a relentless grip, and her head immobilised by a forceful hand spanning her jaw.

'You're a liar, Paige Darling,' he smiled tauntingly down into her apprehensive green eyes with devastating effect. 'And, according to you, that deserves a special kind of retaliation, doesn't it?'

'You mean you'd hit me?' she breathed tremulously, uncertainly. She couldn't really bring herself to believe he meant it.

His thumb travelled tantalisingly over her softly parted lips. 'Oh, no, I can think of something far more appropriate ... and satisfying. Something I should have done days ago,' he drawled, setting his lips on the pulsing base of her throat.

'No, Kelly, no! *Please* don't make fun of me again!' she begged desperately, renewing her efforts to squirm away as suppressed emotions sprang into overwhelming life.

Blazing a trail of desire across her sweetly scented skin, he finally halted at the corner of her trembling mouth. 'I was never more serious in my life,' he advised huskily before claiming her lips completely.

No matter what his answer had been Paige despairingly doubted if her response would have altered in the slightest. She had no will of her own when she was in Kelly's arms. Only an increasing urge to return his deepening kisses with a matching ardour, and to experience again the arousing touch of his exploring, caressing hands. The reasons prompting his actions hardly seemed important any more compared to the way he made her feel!

In a rapturous trance of sensuous warmth she moved beneath him pliantly, arching closer to the hard body which demanded her surrender and, on finding her arms free, linking them about his neck in loving submission. Long fingers deftly disposed of the buttons on her shirt and the fastening of her bra, laying swelling breasts bare to a passionate gaze. The electrifying touch of his mouth as it came into contact with an erect peak sent a quiver of shocked delight surging to the very extremities of her nervous system.

With a feverish moan she clutched at his broad back, the muscles tautly rigid beneath her fingers, as a wave of unrestrained longing swept over her. She hadn't known such pleasure existed, or that she could experience such a depth of feeling, and she didn't want it ever to stop.

It was Kelly who finally called a halt. His breathing as ragged and heavy as hers, his ebony-lashed eyes still filled with a smouldering desire as they scanned her flushed features.

'Either you agree to marry me, or I can see myself losing what little control I have left and taking you right here and now!' he groaned tensely.

Some of the drowsiness in Paige's eyes disappeared—as did all of her inner torment—and her curving mouth widened into a bewitching smile. 'Then I'd better consent while I still have the chance, hadn't I?'

'You mean you'd better consent because you love me,' he corrected, but to her disbelief, not altogether banteringly.

'Oh, Kelly!' Her hands reached up to cradle his face tenderly. 'How could you doubt it? I love you to distraction! I haven't been able to get you off my mind since the night we met, and if you want incontrovertible proof,' she smiled at him mistily, 'just remember I fell in love with a stockman, not a millionaire.'

'*I adore you!*' He dropped a kiss on to the tip of her dainty nose before rolling away to sit with his arms resting on upraised knees. 'But will you ever forgive that little deception of mine, I wonder?' turning to eye her ruefully.

The rearrangement of her clothes completed, Paige cast him a wry grimace. '*Little* deception! I was so hurt, confused, disappointed, and goodness knows what else when I found out who you really were, that I could have killed you!'

'I guessed as much,' he admitted drily, and rubbed a reminiscent hand up and down his cheek. 'That was quite a wallop you let fly with, young lady.'

'I meant it to be,' she confessed with a grin, nestling beneath his arm. 'But I truly am sorry, I shouldn't have done it, I know. At least, not publicly,' she inserted mischievously. 'But if it's any consolation, I felt terrible about it afterwards.'

'Good,' he laughed unsympathetically.

'Beast!' she laughed with him, until a frown slowly descended over her smooth forehead and she queried, 'But why did you lie to me, Kelly? Was it really because you disliked me so much?'

'Oh, God, how wrong can you be!' His arm tightened about her convulsively and he tilted her puzzled face up to his. 'Mistake number one—I certainly didn't dislike you—*ever*! Quite the reverse, in fact.'

'But you said . . .'

A quietening finger was laid across her lips. 'Uh-uh!' he shook his head decisively. '*You* assumed I didn't like you. I merely allowed you to continue in that misbelief by not going out of my way to deny it.' He paused, his expression mock-threatening. 'Mistake number two—I did not lie to you, Paige darling! I may not have disclosed *all* the truth, but I certainly didn't lie.'

Paige was willing to take his word for it, more interested at the moment in discovering with a smile, 'Was that a capital D you just used for my name, or not?'

'Subconsciously, I don't think I've been using a capital for quite some time,' he owned deeply.

A contented sigh ensued, although a few seconds later she still had to probe, 'But why only half the truth? Why not all of it?'

Kelly expelled a heavy breath, his lips shaping into a rueful smile. 'It was a gradual decision, actually. You see, when I met you at the hotel I was highly suspicious of your motives for coming out here— wrongly, I admit, but I wasn't to know that at the time. So, when I also found myself strongly attracted to that selfsame headstrong little redhead, I was quite content to remain the stockman you apparently took me to be—initially, because I found it amusing, but later, because I discovered I could relax and enjoy the anonymity it afforded.'

'Okay, that I can understand. I might not appreciate the reasoning behind some of it, but I *can* understand it,' she acknowledged wryly. 'However ... surely you could have told me who you actually were some time before we arrived at Ainslie! That wouldn't have been asking too much, would it?'

'Hell! How I wish it had been as easy as you make it sound!' he exclaimed ironically. 'But there was I, feeling as if I'd well and truly had the skids put under me ... and I wasn't even sure I even wanted to get married again! And there were you, criticising Bruce Morgan and quoting, "I don't like monopolies," at every turn ... but which I would like to make clear once and for all, it is not! Can you wonder at my reluctance to drop a bombshell of the magnitude my true identity would have been?' He laughed self-mockingly. 'Not having expected you to show any interest in a mere stockman, I then found myself caught in a trap of my own making because I was, quite frankly, too damned scared to tell you the truth in case I lost you altogether as a result of it!'

'And I thought you'd never speak to me again after I slapped you,' she recalled sadly. 'You were so grim that evening all I wanted to do was curl up and die.'

'Yes, well, I wasn't feeling too friendly towards you just then,' he admitted, and kissed her thoroughly to ensure she understood that was all in the past. 'Although I can't say you looked exactly overjoyed to see me either when I asked how you were after that incident with Nadine.'

'Because you went to her first!' she pouted defensively.

'Good lord!' Kelly stared at her incredulously. 'I didn't go to her, you delightful little idiot, she threw herself at me as I was on my way to *you*! All I did was to take her away so she didn't have an opportunity to renew her attack. You don't know Nadine like I do!'

'Happily,' she half smiled, somewhat appeased by his explanation. Her following words had a definite tone of resentment about them, however. 'And was it also to keep her away from me that you've been with her so constantly this last week?'

All of a sudden his eyes gleamed as blue as the sky overhead and his smile had her feeling decidedly weak all over. 'No, that was purely to draw a reaction from you.'

'You succeeded.' She wrinkled her nose at him ruefully. 'I was as jealous as hell.'

'That's what I hoped when I realised you'd started making excuses to stay at the homestead.'

'How did you know they were excuses? Suzanne didn't.'

'Mmm, but Suzanne wasn't with you at Bindaburra, and I've seen you standing in the sun too often and for too long, without it having any adverse effect on you whatsoever, to be taken in by today's effort,' he divulged lazily.

'It still could have been the truth, though,' she persisted.

'It could,' he acknowledged. 'But it was a dead giveaway when I found you with Mercury.'

'Because I was out in the sun again, I suppose?'

He shook his head slowly, starting to laugh. 'Because you were crying all over a horse you don't even like riding! How many clues do you think I needed, Paige darling?'

'Not many, thank heavens,' she smiled up at him starry-eyed, recalling how she had thought the same about Mercury herself. 'Otherwise I would probably still be avoiding you.'

It was too dismal a thought to contemplate and Paige dismissed it rapidly, turning to him with an air of suppressed amusement.

'May I ask you a favour?' she queried, trying to keep a straight face.

Kelly's eyes half closed suspiciously, although his mouth retained its relaxed curve as he lay back on the grass and pulled her down with him. 'Such as?'

'*Please* may I now speak to Stuart?' she laughed helplessly. 'I really don't think there's any need for you to protect him any more.'

'Protect him be damned!' he grinned. 'It's been *my* interests I've been guarding.'

An answer which put an enchanting glow into her eyes. 'Then you will let me talk to him? He must be thinking I'm terribly rude for not bothering to get in touch with him, especially since he was the one to invite me out here in the first place.'

'I'll think about it,' he conceded teasingly, already beginning to reverse their position so that he was leaning over her.

'But not right now,' she vetoed softly, her lips parting to receive his.

'No, not right now,' he averred huskily.

The Mills & Boon Rose is the Rose of Romance

Every month there are ten new titles to choose from — ten new stories about people falling in love, people you want to read about, people in exciting, far away places. Choose Mills & Boon. It's your way of relaxing.

May's titles are:

PAGAN LOVER *by Anne Hampson*
Tara had been forced to marry the masterful Leon Petrides and there was no escape — but did she really want to get away?

GARDEN OF THORNS *by Sally Wentworth*
Somebody was trying to get rid of Kirsty, but she just *couldn't* believe it was the autocratic Squire, Gyles Grantham.

KELLY'S MAN *by Rosemary Carter*
Kelly found it very galling that, despite all her efforts, Nicholas Van Mijden should still persist in thinking of her as just a spoiled rich girl.

DEBT OF DISHONOUR *by Mary Wibberley*
Renata's job was to look after a difficult teenage girl — but she found the girl's forbidding uncle more difficult and unpredictable to deal with!

CRESCENDO *by Charlotte Lamb*
'If you let them, women will take you over completely,' was Gideon Firth's philosophy — and that philosophy had ruined Marina's life.

BAY OF STARS *by Robyn Donald*
Bourne Kerwood had been described as 'a handsome bundle of dynamite' — and that dynamite had exploded all over Lorena's young life!

DARK ENCOUNTER *by Susanna Firth*
'For the salary you're offering I'd work for the devil himself' — and when Kate started work for Nicholas Blake she soon began to wonder if that wasn't just what she *was* doing . . .

MARRIAGE BY CAPTURE *by Margaret Rome*
Married against her will, Claire promised herself that the marriage would be in name only — but that promise was a surprisingly difficult one to keep!

BINDABURRA OUTSTATION *by Kerry Allyne*
'Go back to the city where you belong,' ordered Kelly Sinclair contemptuously, and Paige would have been only too glad to oblige — but fate forestalled her . . .

APOLLO'S DAUGHTER *by Rebecca Stratton*
Bethany resented Nikolas Meandis when he tried to order her life for her — and that was before she realised just what he was planning for her . . .

If you have difficulty in obtaining any of these books from your local paperback retailer, write to:

Mills & Boon Reader Service
P.O. Box 236, Thornton Road, Croydon, Surrey, CR9 3RU.

Doctor Nurse Romances

and May's
stories of romantic relationships behind the scenes
of modern medical life are:

NURSE AT WHISPERING PINES
by Elizabeth Petty
The shock of being jilted had left Storm without the
heart to continue her nursing career. Then she found
that her sick grandmother needed her in Canada —
and so did the uncompromising Clint Hawes ...

WISH WITH THE CANDLES
by Betty Neels
There were plenty of girls with more glamour to
offer a devastating Dutch surgeon than Sister Emma
Hastings. Wasn't she wasting her time by falling in
love with Justin Teylingen?

Mills & Boon Classics

The very best of Mills & Boon
romances, brought back for those of
you who missed reading them
when they were first published.

in

May

we bring back the following four
great romantic titles.

A MAN APART
by Jane Donnelly

Everyone who knew Libby Mason hoped that she and Ian
Blaney would make a match of it, and they were all quick to
point out how misguided she would be to entertain any
romantic ideas about the 'outsider' Adam Roscoe. But wasn't
it just possible that 'everyone' might be wrong?

RAPTURE OF THE DESERT
by Violet Winspear

Chrys didn't trust men, and Anton de Casenove was just the
type of man she most needed to be on her guard against — half
Russian prince, half man of the desert; a romantic combination. Could even Chrys be proof against it?

CHASE A GREEN SHADOW
by Anne Mather

Tamsyn had no doubt about her feeling for Hywel Benedict,
and it was equally clear that she affected him in some way —
but marriage? No, he said. He was too old for her. And there
were — other complications.

THE CRESCENT MOON
by Elizabeth Hunter

When Madeleine was stranded in Istanbul, there was no one to
whom she could turn for help except the lordly Maruk Bey,
who had told her that he found her 'dark, mysterious, and
very, very beautiful.' Could Madeleine trust such a man to aid
her?

If you have difficulty in obtaining any of these books through
your local paperback retailer, write to:

Mills & Boon Reader Service
P.O. Box 236, Thornton Road, Croydon, Surrey, CR9 3RU.

Masquerade
Historical Romances

Intrigue
excitement
romance

THE ELUSIVE MARRIAGE
by Patricia Ormsby

The scandalous circumstances of Cherryanne
Devenish's first meeting with the notorious Marquis
of Shalford made her anxious to forget the whole
incident. Then she found that the more decorous
courtships offered by other Regency bucks had lost
their savour for her . . . .

MARIA ELENA
by Valentina Luellen

A fragile pawn in her father's political game against
Elizabeth I, Maria Elena was torn between loyalty to
him and love for his mortal enemy, Adam MacDonald.
And to Adam she was only an instrument of revenge!

Look out for these titles in your local paperback shop from
9th May 1980